# MIND
# DONOR

MICHELE SCARANO

# MIND
# DONOR

# 1

I live about 14 blocks from the bar but decide to walk. Beneath the underpass, the heavy high-way hum ushers me a block away from home. Turning the corner onto my avenue someone running at full speed crashes into me.

Once I reconnect with my senses I realize I am lying on the ground.

The sky is a marvel of discounted beauty. The change of perspective is quite rewarding but it's only a moment before my brain resets and adrenalin kicks in, tensing my limbs. No pain - only a smothering sensation of being trapped under a person's full weight. A pungent body odour invades my nostrils. I writhe myself free and get back up to discover what just hit me, judging from the smell and the state of her clothes it appears to be someone who has been living on the streets. She remains motionless, so I lean in to discern if she was knocked out or if something more serious happened. Her eyes stare upwards devoid of eyelid movement. My heart races as I brace for the worse, I glance from side to side in search of someone that could help. When my pupils flow back into focus I notice a tear rolling down her temple.

"Are you ok?" I say as she lies there motionless. I ask again, this time kneeling and nudging her on the shoulder.

"Hey! Are you ok?" Her gaze vacillates to the left towards me. She mumbles something I don't understand, then stirs as if trying to get back on her feet. Her body movements are disconnected. I stand behind her, place my hands under her armpits and help her up. Her sweat evaporates on my fingers.

"You should watch where you are going. You almost broke my nose," I grunt as I start registering the tingling sensation spreading from my septum. The woman stands there, dark spatial vacuum in her eyes, as if just brought back by an alien ship. She has thick nutty blond hair, blotched cheeks and yellow lips from too many cigarettes. Lodged behind gold, round, thin glasses lie deep blue eyes, bloodshot above a strong nose.

"I know you won't believe me Vince, but I am here for you." Her voice is rough, as if she has been yelling far too long.

"They are going to take your mind." She holds onto my arm. It recoils under her weight.

"Please, let's go somewhere safe. They are looking for me. For us," the woman pleads.

I wince at her words. Thankfully the grown-up in me simplifies everything: "she is just crazy and you need to get away". I turn around and head home. Crossing the street, I take a quick look to determine her whereabouts and find her right behind me. With each step my heart accelerates, I gawk back and see her on her knees, crying.

Why I decide to stop I don't really know. Possibly because my uncle Frank has roamed these same streets battling schizophrenia. I tell myself to fuck off and turn to retrace my way.

"Listen, can I call someone for you? An ambulance?" I whisper. "Vince, you should not worry about me. It is you I am trying to save." "I don't know you and I can't really hide you; and who should we be hiding from anyways?" I say with a rueful smile. She shields behind her right arm cast across her chest.

"I just need five minutes of your time. I swear you'll never see me again," she pleads. She dries her tears on her coat sleeve, unveiling a Franck Muller watch with burgundy straps. I look down at her shoes. Black Prada sneakers.

The rapids of inertia flow through me on the avenue ahead of me, under towing me, us. My feet grip on the curb's edge, balancing , tipping, falling.

# 2

W̶e get into my apartment, and I have her sit on the couch. Actually I tell her to wait as I spread a newspaper out, and then invite her to kick back. Sitting directly across her, I clasp my hands in front of my face.

"So, who is after you?" I ask trying to pierce through her erratic behaviour.

"How do you know someone is after me?" She abruptly turns towards me.

"You just told me!" A heat rush engulfs me; it was a bad idea to bring her here.

"What's your name?" I urge her. I need to stay calm. If there is someone who is supposed to be sane here, it's me.

"Danielle."

"Ok Danielle. How do you know me?" I enunciate each word to give her time to think about an appropriate response.

"Your name is on the list. They know where you live, where you work, who your friends are. That's how I was able to find you. They know your work number. 914-578-9800," she replies as if it was the most obvious thing in the world. The grin on her face retreats into a frown.

"Danielle you need to be a bit clearer than this. What list?" I harbour her into focus.

She sits quietly, awkwardly raising her fingers to her face as if counting – yet what's most striking is the speed at which her eyelids flinch. Bringing Danielle up was a bad, bad idea but her knowing my name and my direct work line cannot be a mere coincidence.

"Danielle. I am going to the toilet for a second. I'll be right back." Locked inside, I look up the City Angels' phone number. They deal with homeless people all the time. I could tell them I found her unconscious near the building and brought her up to recover. As I am about to dial the number I wonder about my neighbours' reaction if they were to see a group of red berets removing a screaming homeless person from my apartment. The phone slides back into my pocket deciding on an attempt to peacefully get her out myself.

Back in the living room I find her standing on the couch, looking up at the ceiling.

"Hey! Get off! Jesus! This is a brand new Frau from Italy!"

"Did you put the light bulb in yourself?" She enquires sardonically.

"Why?" Why in god's name is she asking?

"You wouldn't understand." Her eyes narrow.

"Have you got a beer at least?" Danielle's demeanour fluctuates from warm to gelid. Once in the kitchen alcohol doesn't seem such a good idea.

"Is Budweiser ok?"

I put the six-pack on the coffee table and sit on the loveseat. My hands are clasped together, elbows on my knees. My feet push my upper body up, pendulously swinging me back and forth like Damocles' sword.

"They know I've found out what they have been doing to me which they will then do to you." Danielle glares into me.

"What do you mean by that?" I stare straight back into her, torn inside. Part of me wants her out and the other is very intrigued; a division which lies deeper into the sinking sands of solitude. Danielle clears her throat - she is about to spit on the floor. "What are you doing? – I holler - possessed by vehemence - For God's sake do it in the bathroom!" I stir on my seat to regain composure.

She stands up and still wearing her camel coat loiters towards the toilet. Staring at the white wall, I imagine myself scrubbing the ceramic bowl with all sorts of cleaning products. As time ticks by my hope of her not taking a shit slowly fades away.

When she finally emerges there is a smile on her face, whilst she scratches the side of her head.

"I know, I was like you at the beginning. I also used to think the people I saw muttering to themselves on the streets were just nutters living on the edge of reality." She leans back on the couch. There is something very familiar about her, but I can't place it.

"What do you mean?" a hint of discomfort and curiosity echoes in my voice.

"Look, not everyone rescues someone like me from the streets. When you and I used to call ourselves normal, we wouldn't have listened. That doesn't mean you'll now start hearing voices like I do, son." She squints her right eye.

"It's more like opening a frequency channel. Finding oneself on a frequency that is hidden to everyone else. It's like the German WWII Enigma code where spies used radio signals to send secret messages to each other."

"Right, and what does this have to do with the people coming after you? I mean us". I am trying not to judge her but my hand is already searching for my phone.

"Remember when you were a kid, life had no time - Danielle's eyes scour the floor and halt to a frown - among all those childhood memories, there are some that are more vivid than others, always alive and ready to come back. This is that channel. Present and past melt together, non-stop déjà vu. It's when you were at home with mum and dad playing with your toys and felt that strange sensation for the very first time. "Has this happened before?"

The head scratching woman goes on, and I am not sure she is making any sense.

"I am a professor of Psychology and I often share a poem with my students by an ancient Sufi teacher Abu-Bakr, called El-Shibli: To your mind, I am mad.

To my mind, you are all sane.

So I pray to increase my madness,

And to increase your sanity.

"Nice. Really. But can we get back to the list. Can you please tell me what this list is about?" I teeter on my seat scratching my mobile's screen with my fingernail.

"I found out I was on the list when it was already too late. But hopefully for you it's not. Then again, I am not sure you have what it takes," says the professor.

"So what will they do to me?" My curiosity turns into frustration; nail jamming into my cuticle.

"They will get into your mind and make you do things you don't want to do." She freezes. I watch her as her hands close into fists. She looks through and beyond me.

"Now, that's something very unpleasant." As my statement floats, silence moves in like a cold front; I tell her to hold that thought to light one up. The search of tobacco allows me to stall for time. When I glimpse at her head, It is tilted backwards as if she had dozed off. With s slightly bent rollie dangling from my lips I press on her shoulder With my index and middle finger. No response. I lean in. Nothing. My finger waits under her nose to check if she's still breathing. Thank God she is. I stand up, glance at my phone and wonder if I should call the City Angels after all. First I decide to go through her coat to find her wallet. I bring it into my bedroom and sit on my lounge chair laying ahead of me a driving license, credit cards, City University badge and about 100 dollars. This woman ain't no bum. Danielle Tom Boban, 13 Pine Street, Tarrytown, NY, NY. DOB: 12/6/1955.

# 3

I am not sure if I've been woken up by sunlight or by the deafening fire alarm. As Danielle's spirit brushes my thoughts, my nerves choke into a knot. I have fallen asleep on the chair. Pulling myself up, my hands hold on to a staggering hope that last night's events are just a ghastly nightmare. Beer cans in the living room are livid images that knock out the hope left wavering. Other images surface, but they belong to a dream. Danielle and I were on the balcony arguing at close range about school grades. Realigning my twisted back I drag myself into the living room. No sign of Danielle. I check the bathroom, the kitchen, but she's nowhere to be found. I slip a pair of jeans and a sweatshirt on and join all the other residents on the way out of the building. The fire alarm keeps pounding my ear drums. Half-dressed tenants, caricatures of themselves, crowd the entrance hall. The suits, skirts and coats I normally share the elevator with are now replaced by sweatpants, bathrobes, shorts, under skirts and yoga tights.

Outside the building someone screams. An ambulance siren blares louder and louder; strident acutes ricochet into a parabolic wall of encroached onlookers. Grazing a crying woman, I make my way towards the commotion, sideways pushing through the huddled bodies when the most disturbing sight I have ever witnessed unravels before me. The woman with whom I was speaking about 5, 6 hours ago is now lying on the ground with a severely fractured skull. The crowd retreats as the pool of blood meanders its way towards me. Her shoeless feet stupefy me.

Did she take her shoes off or it was it the impact with the ground?

Suddenly a surge of nausea clenches my abdomen and I rush towards the curb to reject acrid fluids concocted by my intestines. The building's manager enters my scope when I lean forward with my head, saliva hanging. I wipe my liquids away, get up and run after him to ask what's happened. He tells me that as he was exiting the building he saw this woman hit the ground right before his eyes. His jacket and tie keep his nonchalance compact but his glassy eyes are awash with trauma.

"She must have jumped from one of the apartments or she might have reached the roof" he shudders, looking up at the building. He brings his hand to his forehead, middle finger and thumb pressing his temples. Mirror cells raise my hand pressing on my eyeballs to relieve the pressure.

To get back in the apartment the stairs are a better option as everyone is crowding the elevator. My fingers start tingling as the climb begins; then a sudden, sharp pain stabs my chest. My heart skips and tears. Touching my thorax to determine where the pain is coming from, I locate it near the center of my chest. Blood spreads from ripped heart muscle, flooding the lungs, windpipe and stomach. Cold sweat condenses on my temples, breathing falters, and my hands and feet go numb.

Is this what a heart attack feels like? I don't want to die. Not now. My entire body is paralyzed probably because my heart has stopped pumping. Stretched on the landing between the 3rd and 4th floor, I need to ask for help, but can't move.

Am I just going to die right here? Is this how my life is going to end? I've asked for it and here it is. Wait, someone's coming up the stairs.

"Please help me. I'm having a heart attack." I grab onto his leg.

"What's wrong?" This man, in his 30's, looks like an army guy.

"I can't breathe, and my body is numb. I don't want to die. Please. I'm not sure how much longer I can hold on." I lift my head as much as possible to stare him in the eyes.

"Wait here. I'll get a doctor." I can hear him jump down the stairs, slamming the emergency exit behind him.

"Do you take any medications? Please try to describe where the pain is coming from." The man has a paramedic patch on his shirt. I recognise him. He is the guy who picked Danielle's body up. He pricks my thumb to run a blood oxygen count.

"No medication." He gives me a shot of I'm-not-sure-what and places an oxygen mask over my mouth and nose. As he checks my blood pressure, he asks:

"Do you suffer from panic attacks?"

I shake my head to signal a no.

"Did you just see the body outside?" He smiles bleakly. He then circles me and from behind helps me up to kindly drag me back to my apartment. He sets his medical pack on the table and writes down a full report. He then proceeds to pour some drops into a cup.

"You can keep these in case you feel unsteady." The label on the small container reads Lexotan.

"Now lie on the couch and if possible ask a friend to keep you company for the night. Tomorrow go see your doctor for a check-up. Ok?" the paramedic stares at his watch before collecting his paraphernalia.

"This has never happened to me before" I mumble to him on the doorstep, before locking the door behind me.

Stretched on the couch, mind fucked by what I have witnessed outside, my finger scrolls through the phone screen searching whom to can call or text. Who can comprehend this insanity? Paces lead me to the window. Gravity and fear, huge metal doors which shut me behind my unreliable human. I lumber to the bedroom, pull the handle; wrap myself under the covers; place one pillow behind me, another between my legs. Staring at the white wall ahead, the ivory space is a projection screen of the best hotel rooms I slept in. In the middle of the fourth or fifth sex scene I fade into Puerto Rico.

# 4

---

What happens when you let go of yourself?

One of two things. You either lose touch with reality or you desperately try to let go of the idiosyncrasy you feel no longer works. Honestly, it is unbeknownst to me what I have retained, the only certainty is that which keeps me functioning is being employed at a job. It is imperative I get back to the office if I want to shake this thing.

In the morning sitting in front of our couch unable to absorb Danielle's tragic disappearance - my mind's eye projects her floating apparition. I orchestrate a Sambuca bottle my cousin Anthony left behind, to its left, tobacco with zigzag filters, the drops the paramedic left me and my holy zippo lighter. Thinking has gone circular.

Going to the cops would lift this weight off my chest. Ok. But what would happen if they blame me? The investigation and the prospect of going to jail for murder or manslaughter would be unbearable. Keep thinking. Sitting here long enough could birth a solution that will make it all disappear. Shit. Heroin? Where the hell am I going to get it? Be realistic Vince! Alcohol will have to do for now; and add some of those Lexotan drops. Once the glass hits the table everything goes quiet, thoughts like deep, dense fog abate lingering knee-high Last night's dream creeps up its way in the front hall of my mind. I was an astronaut whose safety cable came undone, left floating into dark, deep space. The vibrating smartphone snaps me back into attention for a text message from a co-worker asking if I will be going into work today. No, I reply. My mind's arms, like those of Shiva, are still trying to pull my shit together and will need this last day to recover. Taking small steps through the living room I lumber into the kitchen to feed myself some cereals. Spoon on the right and phone on the left I scan through the local newspaper for any news articles about Danielle. Nothing. The phone rings in my hand.

"What happened to you?" asks Zac as the reception fades. "Nothing. Just hanging at home. Why?" My wired strung nerves are faster than my words.

"You don't answer my texts or calls. I rang your work and they told me you haven't been there for almost a week! As your friend I think I am entitled to be worried. Aimee wants to meet for drinks and she is bringing a friend, Pearl." Zac's serious tone of voice morphs into collusive indulgence.

"Don't really feel like it," I mumble in reply.

"What's wrong with you?" I can see Zac bend his tongue behind his bottom teeth. A tic he's had as long as I've known him.

"Nothing. I just need to be alone. I think I'm onto something," I say lowering my voice.

"What do you mean?" Zac gets annoyed when I won't be his wingman. "I think I'm feeling different lately, as if I'm changing. I can't explain it."

"What, you found enlightenment? Or is this one of your Zen moments where you ask yourself why you are on this earth?" Zac breaks in that old, familiar laugh I used to hate when he would tease me at John Jay High School. Zac is the rock that keeps me tied down to this reality. He is every day. I am Monday and sometimes Thursday.

"Maybe. It's kind of like that." I say sourly.

"What do you mean? I've told you before you should go to therapy or get into a stable relationship. You can't live alone for the rest of your life." Honesty is the lymph of friendship.

"I am having flashes. Actually, they last a bit longer than that. They're so real that I forget where I am and what I'm doing. I feel really warm all over and all I want is to stay still and stare out of the window."

"You mean you catch yourself talking to people who aren't there? I don't mean to be harsh, but this is so you.

It's like you wished it on yourself." He chuckles and stops speaking for a couple of seconds as if waiting for my reaction. Silence.

"Do you think it's serious?" he retracts.

"What do you mean? That I'm going crazy?"

"Yeah?"

"Well, I don't feel crazy. But then again, isn't that the first symptom of mental illness?" God, I'm amusing.

"Maybe you should see someone."

"What, a psychiatrist? No, it's nothing serious." I need to reassure him.

"So are you going to come out or what? Come on. I can't go alone.

You know how it is. Divide and conquer."

# 5

At the moment it's more divide than conquer. I need to patch this mind split. It bifurcates me. It wants to think about Danielle and keep on trying to figure out what happened. Some fresh air might help. I coat myself with just a couple of Lexotan drops. For once it feels good to be amongst randomness, surrounded by people who don't know a thing about me. Walking down the avenue I search for patterns to route my thinking whilst I keep my body straight to recognize the trajectory. Sifting through human figures that appear on my visual dashboard my mind's eye scans for North Face logos, tracking. At about 88 I realize I have reached Zac's store.

His shop, just off Long Street, is called "Higher Sole". Zac, who is a cobbler, believes shoes represent a window into a person's soul and he backs this up with the evidence that whenever people are killed in major accidents they are inexplicably found shoeless. He showed me a number of photos of tragic accidents such as car crashes, trampling, suicides and it seems to be true, people are found bare foot. Danielle was found without shoes.

The door to the shop is brown with the imprint of letters that have been removed. Together they read Deliveries. As you come in and out of Higher Sole you need to hold the door open to avoid the recoil of the spring that pulls it back. Whilst you descend a narrow corridor through nine uneven steps, you are greeted by a small sign "Head Your Mind." Your hand slides over the smooth wood rail and you land in a small room with a counter on your left, customers shoes on Ikea bookshelves in front of you and more bookshelves loaded with books on your right. Most of the volumes are Zac's, a few are donations from customers. They are mainly self-help and psychology books which you can borrow. In the middle of the room, you can sit at a wooden picnic table, leaf through books and get high on shoe polish fumes. It used to be green but I helped Zac sand it off and paint it burgundy.

In the neighborhood, the word has spread that at Higher Soul not only you get your shoes repaired but you are also offered a free psychological consultation. Zac does not like to be seen as some sort of guru but as long as he can provide people with some good advice he feels he's accomplished something. He told me his theory about shoes was prompted by a book he was reading whilst traveling, "Man and his Symbols" by Carl Jung. If you think of Sigmund Freud as the St. Peter of the mind, Zac explained, Carl Jung can be considered to be the archangel Gabriel.

Zac entertains himself discovering his customers' personalities through an analysis of the creases, tears and wears that appear in their shoes. He picks the shoe up weighing it on his hand as if there were a standard scale to check against. They say a soul weighs 21 grams. He turns the shoe around to gain a broader perspective, then zeros in to take each characteristic into consideration. He compares the wearing of the soles to the appearance of the customer. A man who wears boots and is a pronator - someone who tends to wear their shoes on the inside - will be an introvert who lacks confidence. Then, the more creases are found between the toe cap and the throat line, top of the shoe for the uninitiated, the more issues that man is likely to be dealing with. I remember only too well when Zac first analyzed my shoes. They were burgundy loafers. He said I just hoped to slip in, 'no strings attached.' The old Vince wanted to convince himself of the prospect of a professional career back then, and yes, he was desperately trying to fit in. Ironically Zac, who wasn't trying to fit in at all, would only wear his comfy Birkenstock. He's been wearing the same model since his retreat at a monastery during his life changing trip. Today I am wearing a Dr. Martens steel toe cap safety boot. Humans are unknowingly desperate to connect with others at a deeper level and Zac gives them that opportunity in a simple and harmless way. He demonstrates that if we want to know more about ourselves or about others, all we need to do is to pay attention to the details. Whenever customers ask him to analyze their shoes I don't cease to be amazed by the transformation they undergo. It's not what he says, but the fact that he allows them to let their guard down. It's beautiful to watch and they know they become beautiful. Zac is someone who has taken the time to explore what is out there and has realized it's the simple things that make you happy. It's not about how much money you make; it's about how little you can get away with. "If I gave you soul, what would you do with it? - Zac sings Public Enemy's rhyme as I approach the counter - Hey Vince! Wow. I had to hunt you down and now I get to talk to you twice in a day?" Zac welcomes me, a harmonic smile gleaming in his eyes.

"You right. It never rains, it pours."

"So how have you been feeling? You still having those dreams?" Zac knows where to push. Pressed like a switch, the dream short circuits reality with apparition.

"They aren't really dreams," I correct him. "Since I last spoke to you I haven't had any."

"Well that's good, isn't it?" his forehead wrinkles dissipate on his smile's extended shoreline.

"Sure," I agree as my gaze seems to focus on one particular pair of shoes with a fresh name tag. The right shoe has a standard sole, the left a much thicker one.

"Dude, what's up? What's on your mind?" He stares at me as I pick the fat sole up.

"I don't know. Something strange happened," I admit reluctantly. Friends can be divided into levels of closeness. It's a personal theory. Third level includes the friends you meet and you just hang out with, no emotional attachment involved. You are not going to sleep with their partner because you are a morally sound person, but if you had to, you could. You hang out with them when you feel alone or when you don't have a better alternative.

Second level is made up of the friends you have grown up with. They have always been there and occasionally let you down, but you still accept them because of the past you share. As you grew up you came to discover you no longer have much in common but those memories are like epigenetic DNA traits that you just can't expel. Good or bad, they are part of you.

First level can only exist for friends who keep growing together in life. Most people, after starting their careers become reluctant to explore new areas of interest, like spirituality, philosophy, or art. They concentrate on being successful in their profession and on their family. Anything outside this restricted circle of priorities becomes secondary. Growing together means being able to share and accept the changes you have gone through. What once was a friendship built upon shared experiences becomes a link of mutual respect for having the courage of discovering newly acquired beliefs, ways of thinking and lifestyle choices.

What's on my mind rests entangled between synapses as I decipher whether Zac still belongs to the first level of friendship. Can something this disturbing be revealed without him judging me? Can he be there for me although I have rarely been there for him? Not because I didn't want to but because he hasn't needed me.

"You know I am here for you," he sighs, reading my mind. He smirks, as if suggesting I ought to be ashamed for contemplating the thoughts that just crossed my mind.

"Last night I was walking home and a homeless woman ran into me." I stall for time to consider the best way to deliver this. Something that sounds so fucking absurd to me will probably come across as utterly crazy to him.

"Really? Where was she going? Was she high?" Zac asks.

"She was running from someone," I say as if suddenly believing Danielle's claims.

"Who from? What did you do?" Zac probes me as he stops rubbing a pair of light brown wingtips with his horsehair brush.

"I helped her."

Zac puts the brush down and rests his hands on the border of the counter, his forearms facing me. His eyelids retreat.

"I let her into my home." There you have it. Now I just have to wait for his reaction, hoping he will not leave me alone in this.

"Why?" Zac stays calm keeping his karmic aura. Can the sane understand the insane?

"I don't know. I've been asking myself the same question." I feel my face shrink.

"What do you mean? You let a homeless person into your house and you don't know why?" He looks at me bending his head like a puppy who's heard an acute sound for the first time.

"If someone were in danger wouldn't you help them?" I throw myself a lifeline.

"Well, you did something great, really. But why invite her into your house? Why not just call the cops? Buy her some food? Who knows what that woman could have done to you? Why was she running? Did she tell you?"

"She knew my name." The more I hear myself talking the more I struggle with the thought that Danielle died in my apartment. Well, not in my apartment. Jumping from it.

"She knew your name?" Zac pauses, turns around and places a pair of stiletto boots on the shoe-stretching contraption.

"Could she have asked someone your name? Have you ever seen her before?"

"I had the same thoughts, but she told me we were both in danger. She was running away from some people."

"Yes, from a UFO. Zac chuckles. I see my face beamed in the aluminum glue can."

"Please Zac. I think it was a combination of things that made me believe her. The fact that she knew my name, that she was a university professor, the way she was dressed and just a gut feeling for fuck's sake," I say, looking at him straight in the eyes, hoping to connect with the emotional intelligence I believe he has. When we were kids we used to love going on adventure trips and create a reality where the impossible could happen. We would seek out old buildings' undergrounds or caves to find hidden treasures, secrets. Somewhere inside him that mindset must still be there.

"What do you mean, a gut feeling?" Zac's attention is not waning, but as a practical man he needs empirical proof to take a leap into surreality.

"You know the daydreams I have been telling you about? It's as if they are becoming reality, making the impossible come true. Maybe part of me just wanted to believe her because I am tired of my everyday life."

"Did she say anything else?" Zac's mental dial might be about to find my frequency.

"No. She seemed to be in a stupor. But you haven't heard the worst bit yet." My body quakes As I prepare to confess the unimaginable. The smell of shoe polish fumes blends with metallic blood, vaporing its way into my nostrils. Anger scrapes the bottom of my stomach whilst I outstretch my arms to reach the counter.

"I found her dead at the bottom of my building," I blurt out. Zac stays silent. He grabs his apron to wipe some polish off his hands.

"Zac, I want to cry." It's true when they say a secret needs to stay a secret. It is like a gremlin, a cute creature that, if exposed to water, turns into a monster. A secret, when exposed, undertakes a similar metamorphosis. In your mind it floats between reality and doubt. Then you confide into someone else, and poof, it becomes a ghost taking on solid shape. It is there in front of you, real, heavy, and it slings around your neck like an albatross.

"Ok. Let me get my head around this. You meet a woman you've never seen before, but she tells you she knows you and warns you about someone being after you both. You bring her up into your apartment, and when you are not there she jumps off your balcony and kills herself. Right?" Zac's head mimics my movement as I nod in reply. "Wow. This is some fucked up shit." He pauses and silence hovers overs machines, shoes and all self-help books.

He looks at me. Synapsis connecting and sparking on cortical highway. "Vince look, we could really break our heads over this. I suggest you get away, even if just for a weekend. Go for a trip and try to forget about it. You don't want to get involved in this. My friend is still being summoned to court three years after offering to be a witness to a robbery," says Zac.

"That's easy for you to say. I can't just forget this. I've already been really sick. After seeing the body, I felt as if I was going to have a stroke." I touch my chest just to check if the pain is still there.

"Vince listen, the woman was homeless and probably crazy. You are not responsible for what happened. This is what you concentrate on now. There's nothing you could have done about it, and she probably made everything up to get into the building and jump from it," Zac says, squeezing a plastic Coke bottle. "Are you listening to me?" He pries as he catches me staring into space.

"I know what you need at the moment." Zac comes out from behind the counter, wipes his hands on his apron again, and squeezes my trapezius muscles.

"Is it something that will rid me of that woman's bleeding image?" I writhe in a stream of thought like that of molasses.

"Listen to me. What I am going to tell you may sound like an easy way out but as they say far from the eyes, far from the heart. I mean the mind". – He walks over to the bookshelf, sifts through the volumes and picks up a book with a black cover. He skims the pages and reads:

The LORD says, "Forget what happened before,

and do not think about the past.

I will make a road in the desert

and rivers in the dry land.

My friend slams the book shut and says: "From the book of Isaiah. How about a trip to Vegas so that you can forget what happened? I've always found there is one thing that clears my mind like Zen meditation, and you know what that is." He locks into my eyes and smiles.

# 6

Next morning, at 7:12 a.m. my eyelids retract. I have woken up at least five times since going to bed, I was cold, and then I was hot. Anger and fear grate against each other probably because throughout the night I've been tormented by a nightmare about vampires. In the dream I was flying, circling for prey. If you ask my mother she would say Vince is not the gentlest person, but dreaming of being a vampire is a bit destabilizing. Once out of bed, it takes about 23 steps to the window; the weather outside helps improve my mood. A white billboard held up by thick, solid metal scaffolding has made its appearance on the opposite building's rooftop. In huge Tahoma letters it reads 'Family Time Matters' sponsored by The Ad Council of America.

Today is a good day to get back to work. The thought simmers with a sort of irony since I have come to doubt I can hold off images of Danielle's fractured skull. Almost a week has passed, yet the memory doesn't seem to age.

Turn on the shower, shave my beard, put my blue suit on, gel my hair. In the mirror, I find a decent-looking guy, graying at the temples. Trying really hard not to think about my useless job I walk to the coffee shop next to my apartment.

"A banana muffin and cappuccino?" The Indian barista sees my loyalty and raises her customer service. Whilst the Columbian powder blends on the bulletin board an announcement reads: MWF looking for furnished room.

Smoker, loves animals, Pilates teacher. Come to think of it, I could rent my "office" room and get some extra cash. I jot the number down, let the girl standing in the other cashier line know I'm checking her ass out, and head towards the subway. The moment my foot sets down the steps, a sense of guilt slithers within my thinking. My earlier coffee shop ass peeking regurgitates in my guilt bucket. How would I feel if someone defiled me? This muffin will suffocate me if I don't drink swiftly.

Getting into work is a personal achievement. At the building's entrance, my hand slips into a dignity drop box. Then I unclip my heart to check it with Security. My beta male balls, that's what I ought to unclip. In here, all it is required is the functioning of my reptilian brain. and no (why did you change this?) wonder I am surrounded by snakes. But I am not like my colleagues. Not anymore. My mother is a union member and never speaks well of corporate business.

"A real man works 12 hours in the cold," she says.

My floor sprawls into a huge area partitioned by small space dividers, a labyrinth where rats don't try to get out, but willingly come back in. My cubicle is the farthest away from the corner window and the closest to the emergency exit. Islanded by a bonsai tree, I seat with a fifteen-inch Dell Inspiron and a medal for completing the company's 10K marathon. I had also put up a newsletter article about becoming employee of the month, but it disappeared. Someone must have torn it down, so I replaced it with a Buddha quote that reads 'What we think, we become.' The tools of my trade are a phone, headphones and a computer. My bread and butter is people's peace of mind and for a couple of years I was quite proud of it. I sell health, house, and theft insurance over the phone from 9 a.m. to 5 p.m.

These days, things have changed, I have lost steam. My mother says it has to do with the lack of direction in my life. She promises that if I had children everything would make sense. When you feel stuck times goes by so very slowly; to make my workday bearable I split it into small breaks. At around 9:30 in the morning it's time for my personal email account while eating cereals at my desk. At 11:00, the news online and my Instagram, at 12, before lunch, it's cigarette time. At lunch I read through my favorite sports sites while eating at my desk and then at around 3:30 I drink a Fanta and log onto Facebook. Talking over the phone all day long has developed my visual imagination. Every time I make a call, I imagine what the person looks like, the clothes they wear and the house they live in. Each voice has its own personality and for each one I have developed a strategy to break their defenses down. Cold-calling is what you might call a "calling".

You either have it or you don't; or you have it and then you don't, like me. The manager's role was within my grasps. The contender, a natural, the best in the department because I believed in what I did. It was easy to connect with anyone because I truly had faith that what I was doing meant something, or so I had been able to convince myself. I would speak to listen. Told true stories to back up the importance of what I was selling. My aunt who lost her house to hospital bills, the Zarina hurricane, my friend Zac's house that was broken into twice, my neighbor's sister who died of asthma in her bed. People can feel when you are telling the truth. It must be one of those built-in instincts we have developed through evolution. My passion and conviction improved 12 out of 100 people's lives last year and that's not a bad percentage in telemarketing. Ask anyone in the business.

Now, as with everything else in my life, I have lost thrust. Why? How did (it) come to this? I am not sure. It feels as if I have been waiting for something to happen or as if I have been avoiding something that could happen.

Everyday my colleague Todd sends me a calling list of 'the chosen ones,' the people whose life I can and must change, improve. Over time, I have had to come to terms with the fact that many people don't want to change, so I no longer get frustrated when customers hang up on me.

Simply, they are not ready. With time the similarities with the concept of Karma have become evident. When someone mistreats me, I take it as a manifestation of their Karma, rather than as a behavior directly aimed at my persona. The ways in which we react to life are an expression of the emotional baggage we carry.

"Hello," says Melissa Van Heike, the fifth person on my calling list. She is 28, born in Fishkill, NY and a graduate of Dutchess College.

"Hi Ms. Van Heike, this is Vince Zemolo, and I am calling from Jupiter Network." Never tell them what you're selling right away. You're not from Jupiter Insurance, but Jupiter Network; a word that includes all sorts of interests, ideas and businesses. Don't box yourself in, leave them guessing, hoping.

"Yes?" She offers anxiously. Solitude, modern men's vital resource. An autarchic joke where society creates its own supply and demand. Each dialed phone number is a solitude lottery ticket. There is always a winner. It's a matter of probabilities. That's why we have to call at least 100 people a week.

"Ms. Van Heike, one of your neighbors has requested that we check on your building's safety." Before any call I access our crime news database where we collect local articles about muggings, accidents and fires in each neighborhood.

"Excuse me?" Melissa's tone is the snap of a turtle on flight mode. "I know this may sound like a bizarre question. We are conducting a poll in your neighborhood. Do you think you live in a relatively safe area?" I ask.

"Well, I would say yes. Why are you asking? I do feel safe at home, but I just read that something happened three blocks away from here," Melissa reminisces apprehensively.

"We are conducting a poll that will be presented to the neighborhood council. Prior to the mugging in your neighborhood we had proposed a patrolling service, but you know how these politicians are. It's all about what goes into their pockets," I rally with anti-establishment bravado.

"You got that right, with what we pay for council taxes. Last night I admit I was a bit scared after watching Panic Room. You know, that movie about a break-in, with Jodie Foster. Today on my way back home I found myself paying attention to particulars I wouldn't usually notice, like my neighbor's door handle being broken, for example."

"Oh yes, I also watched that movie last night. I am big fan of Jody Foster, but I have to admit I found the film a bit claustrophobic; shooting an entire movie in one house only. She is really good, but she has done better work. I was actually surprised to see her in a mother role, being a lesbian and all" I say, pleased with my insight. Then I feel warmth spreading on my cheeks.

"That's true, but she's good like that. She can play any role," Melissa snarls with proud female's camaraderie.

"It reminds me of a girl I used to date who turned out to be a lesbian. Sorry, you probably did not need to know that." A few seconds of silence pass by. I might have, no I have, overstepped my professional boundary.

"Really? That must have been tough. Well, I've found myself in a similar situation." She seems genuinely moved.

"It was tough, although I've realized it was what I needed at that moment of my life. I mean, two people are attracted to each other for a reason and that might not necessarily be love or the desire to have babies," I say.

"How is that?" Melissa's interest doesn't wane. I shouldn't get too personal but God does it feel good to be the one to be heard for once.

"At the time I was coming out of an important relationship and I was afraid of getting close to someone. What better way to ensure things wouldn't work out?"

"Self-sabotage is not always a bad thing," Melissa offers.

"Sorry, I'm rambling." As I stare at my desk, small black marks begin to appear on its white surface. Gradually they morph into numbers. I realize I have six more calls to make.

"Oh, don't worry. It's not that easy to entertain a decent conversation these days."

"Well I agree and it's great when you can have a worthwhile exchange, especially over the phone. I actually have to reach out to a few more people to ensure we can get the council to make a move. It would be really helpful if you could support us with a contribution of $45 to set up a neighborhood watch organization. Do you think you might be able to help?" With regret, I force this last phrase out of me transacting humanity for commercial gain.

"How about we continue our chat over a cup of coffee or a cocktail?" says Ms. Van Heike. Speechless, I scroll down my prospecting script without finding an appropriate answer.

"Well. Sure. That would be a first." I am startled.

"Ok. We could go to Trotsky bar on Fielding Avenue tomorrow." How quickly can the tables turn. I was pitching and now delightfully enjoying catching.

"Yes, sounds great. Hold on. How will I know what you look like?" I ask refraining my excitement.

"I am blond and I wear my hair in two pony tails. That should make it easy for you to find me."

# 7

Next day, preparing for my date, the goal is to rummage through my closet in search of clothes that bear no resemblance whatsoever to the ones a telemarketer might wear. What does a telemarketer look like, anyway? Black jeans, black Air Jordan Rising High, black cotton turtleneck, and a black leather jacket. Unable to find that blue scarf my ex bought me, I riff through my closet and below the sweaters at the bottom, there is an old duvet cover. Both arms outstretched, I carry it to the living room, take a deep breath, unfold it and lay it over the couch. May Danielle rest in peace.

Arriving at Trotsky Bar early enough allows me to walk by it a couple of times. It's a brown building with wood-framed windows. The place appears to be full, but I can't quite see through the fogged-up windows. Inside, my pupils delate against the warm and sticky air whilst my jacket seems to decompress on me. I breathe a few moments to settle in. My visual radar scans through each table to find my pony-tailed date. In the corner, between the band and the hallway leading to the restroom, is a blond woman sitting alone. I study her profile from a distance, lingering on her straight nose and on her pronounced lips. Her legs are crossed, thin, wrapped in black tights under a short jeans skirt and black boots up to her knees, her hair is split in two ponytails. A vaguely erotic ogle rests on her face as I walk towards her; I can't help wondering why such an attractive girl would be willing to meet a total stranger. I start to have second thoughts and feel like turning back. Just as I slow down to retreat, she turns in my direction, I smile, keep approaching and lean in: "Hello, are you Melissa?" I ask, one hand in my jeans pocket, the other holding my jacket.

"Yes. Are you Vince?" she enquires with a smile, looking more excited than I would have expected. Maybe she likes what she sees.

"Yes. Have you been waiting long?" I slide on the chair.

"I came about twenty minutes ago. I like the music here, so I came early on purpose," she says with an overly mature tone that confuses me. "Sometimes I actually come here alone," she goes on.

A man should be thankful for the existence of this kind of free-willed women. They are the ones you can expect release from but hope not to marry.

"I like jazz a lot too. I've been here a few times." I desperately need to get a drink. My diaphragm cramps, further contracting with each breath A waiter passes by but by the time I ask Melissa what she would like to order he's gone.

"I actually tried to catch his attention earlier, but he might have figured I was waiting for someone," she says, smiling at me. I steal a glance at her, trying not to seem too interested. She appears mature, yet very young. The wrinkles around her eyes reveal an "almost-thirty" age, but her demeanor is of someone younger. To break the tension I wave the waiter down once more.

"So what did you do last night?" I ask a laid-back question to ease into some kind of conversation.

"Oh, yes. After our call I went out for dinner with a friend, then I did some research on a project I am working on. What about you?" she asks, squinting.

"Nothing much. I went over to a friend's house to eat tiramisu, and then we played on the XBOX. Where do you work?" I am a bit unsure about my comment. Gray hair and video gaming.

"I'm doing a PhD at City University. By the way, I have an XBOX too, and I'm still trying to finish Assassin's Creed Syndicate."

"You're kidding! I just finished it and the ending is not as cool as the whole game. It kind of let me down. Where did you get to in the game?" I don't ask about her PhD as I am embarrassed by my lack of a university degree.

"I am at the point where Henry warns the Frye twins that Starrick plans to break into Buckingham Palace. It's actually pissing me off because I've done it about 100 times now and can't get any further." I start to laugh, as her innocence is too cute.

"Sorry, but I just find it so cool that you are playing my same game. You just don't seem like the type. I love to be surprised. It's a bit hard on the ego, but it gladly reminds me that in life I can't make assumptions after all." I comment.

"I agree. As they say, appearances can be deceiving." Her eyebrows stretch upwards.

"Very true." She is turning out to be someone I can't pin down. She is sexy, quick, and plays XBOX. Is this what attraction is about? Wanting what we don't know and consequently don't have? Is it greed? As defined bodies we can't absorb what we don't have, so we surround ourselves with it.

"How about you? Anything about you that could be classified as deceiving?" Melissa asks as she takes a sip of the drink that was so hard to get.

"Well," I say, buying time to delve into my memory RAM. Self-defying Images of situations, sensations, sounds, manifest before my mind's eye. Anamorphic, reflected on my glass, , it's not actions or reactions. It's what's inside it, me. Like a glass, what is important is what it contains, not how it is shaped or how unbreakable it is. But forget pop philosophy or falling in love. it's about getting laid. Of course, this is all well and good but before words come out of me a shadow starts throwing paper-like images wrapped around rocks into my consciousness. Don't you forget me. Danielle is here and she is drinking my same damn beer.

"Lately I have been losing consciousness." Well, the choice to keep it light has not gone very far. My mouth carries on.

"What I mean is not that I find myself somewhere without knowing how I got there. It's more like day-dreaming in front of my window, but a bit more intense than that." I feel Somehow relieved by a simple explanation to hide something that is really bothering me. Lying on our first date doesn't feel right. It's been a long time since I have been out with a woman I really like.

Melissa, hands clenched together, leans forward and with excitement says, "Tell me more." I am positively surprised because I have never met a woman willing to dive into my emotional vacuum. They have reached for my heart, but ended up drowning into my psyche.

All of the sudden, the music stops. The band takes a break, and unease fills in the void, making my speech flat, staccato. I excuse myself for the Gents. There is no bowl movement but when the tension builds up my intestine acts up. The roll of toilet paper is just about enough to cover the seat and some more; adjusted on the seat, the door stares back.

John was here. 9/05

Meet me at San Fernando, 1 617 888 2367.

Life is duality. Love is the bridge.

YWM, 10inches, 889 921 7899

Now if that pen was still in my pocket. As my stomach decontracts something racks out of my brain.

"Man is mind and body. What we create with one disappears. What we create with the other lies here."

Walking back I become aware that I have taken longer then usual to relieve myself How would Melissa picture me sitting on the toilet bowl I wonder. Back at the table my arms elongate on the surface and my gaze angles towards the band, trying to regain composure. Melissa acknowledges me for a second and goes back to following the music. During the next interval she asks me to finish explaining about my "day-dreaming."

"I can be at home looking out of the window, and all of the sudden I see myself on a beach, and I experience the exact emotions I would feel if I was there."

"I have had something similar, but without losing connection with my surroundings. During the day I have gone through the same sensations I had previously felt in a dream. It's a bit like an emotional flashback." Melissa leans on the back of the chair and continues.

"It's all about your own perception of reality, after all. When I see someone talking to themselves on the street, I think they might have accessed a reality that is invisible to us."

I look covertly at her. knowing I shouldn't, but when something sounds and looks so good it tends to have a hypnotic effect on me.

"That's interesting," I say to stall for time whilst I think about what I will say next.

"I've never looked at it that way. There is such a stigma on mental illness that it makes you hide anything that might not be regarded as normal even from yourself." I say.

"I don't think people express what they feel enough. It is the fear that if you let out what's inside you, you'll no longer be able to stop it," Melissa says pursing her lips. Like a satellite in an elliptic orbit, I pull my chair next to hers to shift our attention to the band.

I sit quietly trying to follow the beat, Satisfied with our discussion and with the impression mirrored on her face. Music is like a kiss on a first date. You talk and talk to hide the tension, then at once you kiss, the tension becomes background. At around 1 a.m., we walk to the subway and agree that we would love to see each other again. She nods and I lunge in to kiss her on the cheek.

# 8

Walking home, I appreciate again what it feels like to share time with a woman. It's been a while since Jenny, my ex, has moved out. Images of Danielle start circling me like prostitutes in a Bangkok Hallway. I now realize that to stop thinking about Danielle I need to concentrate on that very sensation that takes over all others. Sex is the only sustainable way to shut the obsessive thinking off without hurting myself. Not heroin, alcohol or food. I know this because whenever I would feel depressed during my college years sex was the only activity that had the power to pull me out of it. I did try drugs but it would make things worse. Part of me would welcome the ritual to score it, to set it up, to smoke it. For a couple of hours it would cover the loneliness, the sense of lack of accomplishment or reason to be. But another part of me would then desperately grab hold of the high sensation without letting go. The high would persist much longer than expected and I would panic, dreading I would not be able to get back to a normal state of mind. It was like being in a waking coma. Watching as the world moved on, whilst I was trapped in my persisting altered state. Shifting from believing to be the deepest person on earth, to alienating relaxation, fretting anticipation and endless dissociation. Sex also has a ritual, a clear objective, and an assured high with a guaranteed conclusion only I can control. No sense of detachment or panic attacks.

When I am about to reach my building I take my phone out to text Melissa about the great time I just had and find out she's written already.

Vince,

I wanted to tell you I had a lovely time tonight and was thinking it would be nice to meet again.

Call me soon.

Melissa xxx

When I get back home, I sit on the couch and turn the TV on. I grab my phone and start scrolling through my Instagram account. Photos of airplanes, hipster bikes, breakfast plates and unfortunately that lingerie model. Like a bulimic person who's triggered to eat by a TV ad, I head to my bedroom.

Next day, at work, after a birthday party and a department meeting update, I find myself doing something completely out of character. Unlike my usual attitude (never look too interested) I don't waste any time and at lunchtime I dial Melissa's number.

"No!! Stop! This is ridiculous! She's going to think you are desperate . Just wait! Let's see if she writes again. That way we can be sure she is really into us and we will avoid looking needy and stupid. Do I have to think of everything?"

"No. I just want to do what I feel like doing."

"You know that things don't work that way. It's all about first impressions."

"Hi Melissa, its Vince." I have always felt self-conscious on the phone, but when you figure that being in someone's company makes all the bad stuff disappear, you make the call. Even if it means having to endure a relentless voice that screams louder and louder in your head.

"Hey there. Long time no speak." She sounds happy to hear from me and continues:

"Did you sleep well? Any nightmares about a strange 2 pigtailed blonde?"

"I went to bed really late. I stayed up all night watching Masters of Sex, you know the series."

"Yes. It's quite good. Why couldn't you sleep?" As her question floats through the ether I try to imagine what she looks like when she is alone in her house. What does she wear? Is she messy? My mind stands still whilst my gaze wanders across the living room. I find myself lingering on the Blanc, Bleu and Rouge DVD trilogy with French actress Juliette Binoche, directed by polish director Krzysztof Kieslowski. As my eyes get stuck on the shelf, images of Danielle's body slowly stain my retinas, shriveling like burning camera film.

"I often spend hours online finding out about the most obscure subjects," Melissa says.

"That's the great thing about the web. It's like asking God a question. The web is better than any religions out there. You ask for help and you actually get it. What miracle are you asking for, Melissa?"

"You are probably right Vince. We have access to so much information that if we use it in the right way we can make miracles happen, especially in science." Melissa replies.

"Do you use the web for your research?" I ask.

"As a matter of fact I do. I have been working on an online community project for my degree."

"Something like Facebook?" I am more and more captivated by this woman. The contrast between her physical innocence and her intricate mind is causing me to want her more and more.

"Well," she pauses. "It is not a normal type of community." "What do you mean?" I emphasize the last word to underline my interest.

"I mean it is not what you would consider a classic social media community site like Facebook or Twitter." She pauses as if wondering whether I would be able to understand her, or maybe she just doesn't feel like talking about work.

"It's a research project."

"What kind of project?" I push her a bit as the digital world fascinates me. If I could go back in time and have a chance to go to university, I would try to make it a career.

"It's actually an app where people can post requests for casual encounters." Melissa's tone of voice lowers considerably; she is afraid of my judgment.

"What kind of encounters?" This is too good but I need to stay cool.

"Well, the ones where people meet up to have a good time. You know…"

"That's funny," I say to ease the awkwardness.

"You see! I shouldn't have told you!" she says in that pretending to be angry kind of way.

"Sorry. I meant funny as in interesting. Very interesting."

"The app is actually pretty successful. Lots of people are downloading it," says Melissa.

"I bet. What's it called? " I reach for my iPhone in my pocket. I recall reading on Wired about Grinder app, a geo-locating app that allows to find people around you who are interested in sex; but it's targeted to the gay community.

"AppYours. At the moment it's only for iPhone, we are working on the Android version."

"Nice and direct. I like it. What kind of people sign up?"

"At first we thought it would only attract weirdos but the turnout we have had so far has been amazing. It's mainly people that range from 28 to 45 years of age," says Melissa.

"What do you get out of it? Meaning what is return on investment?" I imagine developing an app must not be cheap.

"The app is free, but those who sign up are required to anonymously comment on their encounters. Since the app is funded as a university project the return is the Q&A sessions we engage our members with."

"So have you acted on any of the requests?" I try to sound as detached as possible.

She pauses and says, "Well, if I told you that, I would have to kill you." After this cul-de-sac statement I decide to put it in reverse and wait for her to change the subject.

"So do you still want to hang out with me?" Her voice is soft and gentle.

"I told my friend Zac I would go and see him tonight. Are you free on Friday?"

"That's too bad. I was going to take you to a seminar on digital eroticism. The professor holding it is the one who is overseeing my project."

"Sex and books. That's every student's dream. I should really go back to school." We end the call with an agreement to catch up on What's App to decide on a time that suits us both. I then go on to open Melissa's Facebook profile in search of a photo that reveals her body. I go through all of her albums and only find this one picture of her wearing a bikini.

# 9

A t about 9pm I go out to meet Zac. Walking down a new street parallel to the one I usually take. I want to make damn sure I avoid the place where I crashed into Danielle. A smell of wet cardboard reminds me of something I can't place it, but it fills my chest with a sense of belonging. It starts to rain, it's actually pouring, so I pop into a grocery store to find shelter. Through the first aisle; on my left is a long open fridge for vegetables and on the opposite side is a glass window overlooking the street. Outside the cars' red and white lights leave temporal streams. A glimpse of my reflection appears which I quickly s leave behind when I turn into the next aisle. t In the canned goods aisle I think about a news article in which the journalist argues that it is easier to meet a woman at a grocery store rather than at a bar. At a grocery store people seem to be less guarded. A quite attractive girl slowly pushes her cart, my lack of confidence reminds me that my reality is not contemplated in the article. Tail between my legs, I head towards the door where It's only drizzling now. I walk about 2 more blocks and I get to Gordon Street, number

59; the bar's yellow neon light reads 'Medina.' Whenever I am going to meet someone I like to get there first. It helps me to better savor what will happen. It's like painting. First I frame the environment and then I focus on the subject. I open the door and it feels as if everything is happening in slow motion. It's a midweek night, and the bartender is busy cleaning the mirror behind the counter. As she turns around to look at me, her dreadlocks follow her head movement; they keep on swinging after her head stands still. She stares into mid-air, not directly at me, and then looks down and goes back to her cleaning. I walk across the narrow entrance between the counter and the wall to get to the tables in the back room. As I choose my table, I notice a couple opposite me, probably on a first date, overly concentrated on the conversation. Both upper bodies lean on the table and like a gift-wrap ribbon the girl's red thong appears above the waist of her low-rise jeans. Next to the couple, still tanned from a recent vacation, are 2 blond girls swiping photos on an iPhone 13 . They are locomotives of words, huffing and puffing on their electronic cigarettes.

I can't be bothered to take my jacket off; I sit down, hands hermetically sealed in my pockets. What can I do not to look alone? I sit sideways on the chair and lean against the wall. A Japanese couple comes in and sits at the table next to mine. Right behind them the waitress comes over to ask if I would like to order something. I recognize Baby Alpaca's Vodka Lemonade over the sound system.

"Vodka Lemonade, please."

The female bartender, like all attractive city women, has a savoir-faire of inaccessibility. I stare at her to make her feel uncomfortable and when I feel satisfied, I reach for my cell phone. As I am about to check the time, a draft of cold air ushers Zac inside. Again, time seems to slow down and actions appear in frames. 1st frame. The bartender is turning towards the door as she pours a drink for a guy at the counter. 2nd frame. The waitress is placing beers on her tray. 3rd frame. The blond girls are staring at a bracelet. 4th frame. The Japanese guys are toasting each other.

When I see Zac's friends, Aimee and Pearl, I wonder which of the two girls Zac is interested in. One of them is tall, with wavy blond hair and a long face. The other one is shorter, with black curly hair. The former for sure. Zac reaches the table and squeezes my shoulder as he walks around me to sit down. I know what he is thinking.

"Hi, I'm Vince." I stretch my smile to ensure I come across as a nice guy as possible.

Simultaneously Zac says, "These are Aimee and Pearl." Aimee, the blond, has really fair skin, a high German forehead and long fingers. Her legs are crossed; two long Hugg boots cover her skinny jeans. She sits on my left, while Pearl is on my right hand side. Pearl's hair is jet black, really curly and long. She might be of Israeli or Arabic descent. I imagine her nipples to be much darker than her friend's. She has green eyes and a mole on the right side of her neck.

"Have you been here long?" asks Zac.

"Got here about 5 minutes ago, I think. Did you drive?" "No, we took the subway from uptown."

Zac asks if we want something to drink and goes off to the bar. I feel pressured to start the conversation and avoid us sinking all into our cell screens. I want to say something but the memory of Danielle is weighing me down. I know girls like funny guys. Guys who can make them laugh and release the tension. I am not funny. I try. I really do. I quickly get up and make it look like I just received a call. I start talking to myself whilst I walk towards the entrance and wait for Zac to get back to the table.

"I shouldn't be here. But I guess better here than at home." "We really can't fuck this up for Zac. Stay focused. Think pussy."

I head back once Zac has returned to the table.

"So how did you get to know Zac?" I ask the girls as I pass them the drinks from his tray.

Aimee reaches out for the drink with her long branches and says "We used to go to Qi Qong class together and Zac was the guy that always came late. Then one day we both arrived late and found the studio door locked. So we went for tea and got to know each other."

I want to continue the conversation but I don't have anything else to say so I rely on my buddy to do the talking and cover my somberness with his light-heartedness. I remember Zac when we were kids. I was the one fighting back the kids that would call him a "chink" for his French-Japanese eyes. That which at 10 years old looks mismatched becomes harmonic beauty at 30.

"So you made it out? You growing a beard?" Zac tries to electroshock me out of my emotional shadow.

"Honestly, I haven't actually looked in the mirror in a while." Feeling relatively self-conscious I take out my cell below the table. I open the photo app and select the reverse mode to look at my reflection.

"You know sometimes I feel I look good, and other times I don't. It's kind of strange. Do you guys ever get that?" The girls look at Zac as if to ask him to translate what I just said. Aimee is waiting for Zac to react. He smirks, knowing too well I am not the best at first dates.

"Actually, sometimes I get that," Aimee surprisingly connects with me.

"Don't they say that beauty is in the eye of the beholder?" says Pearl, resting her wrists on the edge of the table and tilting her head slightly on the right side.

"I agree. I think that beauty reacts to our hormones. I will never forget falling madly in love with this chubby girl no one wanted to date. It's not that being chubby is not attractive but it was the first time I felt under an a hormonal spell." I say.

Zac turns from beer to rum and I follow his example to loosen up.

Pearl, a social media manager, brings up a Dove commercial in which they conducted a social experiment using an FBI forensic artist to prove that women often hold a distorted perception of themselves.

"In the experiment they compared the drawings freely created by the expert with those he produced starting from the women's self-descriptions. Can you guess what the result was? Women tend to find themselves uglier than they really are!" Says Pearl as if presenting in front of a client.

Aimee replies "Oh yes, I have seen that video and found it quite striking. Perception is a strange thing. It's like when you buy a car and you love it. Then after a while, as with anything, you realize the design is not as amazing as it seemed 1 year earlier." Aimee looks down at her palm as if contemplating her statement further in her own hand but stops. I continue.

"When I was dating my last girlfriend sometimes I would feel she was beautiful. But at other times I would just feel the opposite way. To this day I can't understand why that happens." I probably got a bit too personal with this statement and Zac, who knows I can be a party pooper, steps in.

"I told you there was a bug in your Google Glasses!" Zac brings two of the semi empty glasses to his eyes to mimic the eyewear and some of the ice falls on the table. I watch the ice cubes slide in different trajectories. One falls in Pearl's lap, another between my legs and a third beneath the blond girls' table. Pearl's red nails clench the cube to bring it back into the glass. She wipes her fingers on her skirt and then slowly slides her thumb on her fingertips to feel the cold reaction on her skin. After the commotion Pearl gets up to use the ladies' room and I go after her. She is wearing purple ballerinas. As she is about to approach the bathroom she turns towards me but I swiftly enter the Men's. We both know we are here for our friends and when we meet up at the sinks I suggest we leave together and let the others continue the evening. Back at the table I share our intention and Zac is great at pretending to look upset. Aimee asks Pearl to go back to the bathroom with her and after a 5 minutes consultation Pearl and I get out of the bar with a clear destination in mind, home. She's not shown any interest in me so I don't bother stressing over to ask her number. I got someone waiting for me. A formless creature, in the back of my head, waits to be dealt with. As I walk Pearl to the nearest subway, I manage to make small talk and think of ways to shake the formless dark presence. I ask Pearl how long she's known her friend for, where she works and what her job is. Wasted words to me but cartilage to an emotionally atrophied human race. On the train back home my head is bursting. The creature is spurting through my orifices. I hear it scream when I am suddenly jolted by the train exchanging tracks.

# 10

I would say my most developed sense is smell. Back home, when I open the door a peculiar scent is awaiting for me. My first response is to think of it as just being the fruit of my imagination but the smell reminds me of my mother. It's strange a mix of her perfume and Danielle's body odour and cigarettes. I'm pretty sure I haven't smoked in the house this morning and I am told my sweat's odour is not very strong. Honestly, I might be imagining it. At least this is what the empiricist in me is saying. But my spiritual side is triggering my anxiety as it remembers a friend explaining that a pungent smell is a clue t of a haunted house. Haunted or not, I am facing a feeling similar to the one I experienced when my house was broken into two years ago. It can be summed up as loss of trust. Your intimacy has been violated and you can no longer call it home. This must be the reason why Zac's suggestion to take some time off shoots into my brain like a geyser.

"Yes. I need to leave the apartment. I need to get this smell off of me. "

"We don't have much money, so it will have to be a nearby destination. Anything but here will do though. Sure, go. But I doubt any of this will go away."

"God. I need to stay positive."

"Yeah, keep it together Vince!"

Instead of checking my mails I get on the App Store and look for Melissa's app. If it isn't heroin sex it will be the way to keep my anxiety at bay. Sex, and masturbation in its weaker form, are the most underrated version of an addiction. I can picture the pleasure centers in my brain being stimulated, endorphins being released into my bloodstream to trigger that feeling of relaxation, accomplishment and harmony.

I go on the App Store website and search for Melissa's app AppYours. I find something with the same name but lacking an s at the end. It has a black logo with a white arrow in the middle. The description reads:

"Don't have a way to tell that special one to go to hell? Build a 'wish well' card with our custom engine. We provide you with the photos and with the best lines from the top and angriest copywriter in the advertising industry to send off to your 'loved' ones."

I swipe down to check the next result and find what I believe is the right app. The app icon is made up of a gold screw and bolt. Below it are 4 screenshots of the app with text describing it. The first one shows multiple profiles of men and women, some fully clothed, others semi naked. - The copy reads 'Find the perfect match, wherever you are, whenever you want' - The second one is a full image of a profile with a heart icon, a thumb down icon and a chat icon - 'Find your match Like, Dislike or Message each profile' -the third screenshot is made of ratings and of comments the community has given to the member - the copy reads ' see what the community says about this member performance and satisfaction - the fourth screen is about the personal details required to find a match - the copy reads 'List your preferences, what you are into, what you are good at, your personal attributes.' AppYours seems similar to Tinder, with an adult sexual twist.

I click on the GET IT link and wait for the app to download. When it finally appears on my mobile screen it requires me to register. I fill in all of my regular data, age, date of birth, email, password. Unlike other social apps it requests very personal questions which at first I feel uncomfortable with but then go on to fill in so that I can get the best out of the service.

Nickname: Vomolo

How long are you? Short/Medium/Long/XL

How thick are you? Small/Medium/Large/XL

Are you circumcised? Yes/No/Can't say

How many times can you come in 1 night? 1/2/3/4/5

Do you do cunniculingus? Yes/No/Sometimes

What are you in for? 1 on 1; 2 on 1; Group; Voyeur

How often do you view porn?
Daily/Weekly/Monthly/

What % of sexual partners was met on the net?
10/30/50/70/100%

As I go on to answer all the questions on the list, a strong sense of belonging fills me up. Other people out there, like me, need to connect and to forget.

Once I am done revealing my intimate details, I'm asked to select an image of myself. I am undecided on what to choose but I I'm sure of one thing, I won't use a naked pic. I settle for one where I am riding, topless, my bike in Venice Beach. To complete my profile I pick a nickname and write a short bio. Do people actually read these things?

Nickname: Vomolo

"Hello World.

Tonight looks like an amazing night. Ready for a great dinner and some great Barolo wine at mine?"

When I realise I have overrun my break time, I shut the app down. get back to check the call list and start dialing.

At 11 o'clock, I can't sleep so I access the app again. A small banner appears and asks me to geolocate myself. Once I agree to terms and conditions of sharing my location, small profile images start to load up on the homescreen. They include a photo and the sexual preference we share.

As I swipe through profiles, I notice that the fourth one shows a red dot over the inbox icon. This person has sent me a direct message. The profile image reveals a woman with curly blond hair in a white dress holding a champagne glass. In the background is a beach and, beyond it, deep blue water. The woman is sitting on a beach bed, leaning forward to show her plentiful cleavage. A big, round white straw hat covers her face. Her message reads:

DawnFuss 35 Years

"Hey Vomolo, I also live on the east side. Would love a glass of Barolo. What time and what's the address?"

I click on her photo profile to find out if I can discover more about her appearance. All of her other images are body shots which reveal a pretty fit body. I have used online dating sites before and know that if women are not in shape they will not include a full body image in their profile. The chance to experience pure pleasure without the burden of emotional involvement sparks an adrenalin rush that pushes the lingering sense of doom away.

I am desperately trying to avoid the couch area. I prepare a salad and eat it in my bedroom. I watch the second episode of the first series of True Detective with Matthew McConaughey and Woody Harrelson. Once I am done with eating I go back to the kitchen, open the cabinet above the dishwasher and grab a bottle of rum which I never thought I would drink. I won it at a work Christmas sweepstake and kept it for that housewarming I never gave. I take 2 big swigs and lay my head down on the pillow. As I look up I relish the bitterness on my tongue, the burning sensation in my throat and the warmth down my stomach. That same warmth my dog would seek during wintertime by getting as close as possible to the wood stove. I sleep off into unconsciousness remembering it groan as it laid there, wrapped around itself.

# 11

I get into work early to call some car rental places. I set up a pick-up for 9 a.m. the next day. I am not really sure where I am heading to but before anything else I want to t make sure I can afford it. As I get off the phone, my colleague Todd, who has pleasantly overheard my call, comes over to my cubicle and asks where I intend to go. He tells me he is free this weekend and would love to get out of town. I have known him for a year and half but only as a colleague. He is an ok guy. We have had some good conversations over lunch. Todd is what I would call a good listener. He lets me do all the talking and unlike my usual self I take advantage of it. I need the self-esteem boost. Getting back to the trip. Although I like the guy I do have some reservations about spending a whole weekend with him. Then again, considering the level of anxiety I seem to be falling into, it would probably be better not to be alone. I know Zac has to work so I don't bother asking him. Todd and I agree to go to Atlantic City since neither of us has been there before and it's a place where we can be independent of each other if we need to be. I have never gambled before, but some crazy lights, betting, and hookers might help me think less about all that's happened.

In the morning, before heading out I feel very tense. Again, I didn't sleep well. Danielle pushed her way into my dreams. We were talking on that goddam couch. She seemed ok, she was asking me to come and join her geology course back at my high school in Rome, New York. Then, she suddenly turned her head exposing her fractured skull. She said, "I have a cavern I'd like you to explore." I haven't been able to take a shower, I am so tense. I go in the kitchen and pour myself some more of that rum. I feel slightly better.

I arrive at the car rental place at 9 a.m. sharp. CARYOURENT is not AVIS and you can tell by the fact that the office is situated on an elevated trailer. In the car lot I can see a fairly random fleet. I don't spot any new cars. I walk up the three stairs to the trailer. I am greeted by someone who behind the counter is eating noodles out of a foam container. He is a young Asian man, probably Chinese judging by the red strings onto which a jade Buddha dangles from his neck. He has fair skin and some facial hair just above the end of his lips that makes him look 15. He has long fingers and a long pinky nail on his right hand. He is wearing a white short sleeve shirt with a blue tie. Behind the counter there is a poster of a blond smiley woman promoting Omniprise Insurance. The poster is tearing at the top. The Chinese man hands me the contract and insurance papers. The car I am offered is a Ford Focus about 3 years old. After having loaded my luggage, I connect the stereo/audio cable to my iPhone and message Todd that I'll be at his place in 20 minutes.

Once on the highway I push the car to max and the speed dial does not go over 80 mph. Todd is much too excited, starts going through my Spotify selection, asking me what my favorite music is and when I listen to what. I look down at his shoes. He is wearing black Timberland-like boots.

"I've always wondered what people with 'Jesus Saves' stickers on their cars are like," Todd says as we overtake a brown station wagon. "Are you religious?" he asks, his face turning away from me.

"I believe in a God that does not interfere in our lives. He is everything. Not sure if any man was ever directly in contact with him. He is definitely not in contact with me i, although I admit to having asked for his help." I grab the steering wheel with both hands and squeeze it to pull my body up. I continue. "In my opinion most of us replace God with things like a family, a child, a lover, a job, a dog, a house. Finding God, I believe, is becoming self-sufficient on your inner source of love where you no longer need but have and want to share it." I speak.

"Sounds like you know what you are talking about. It seems you found your own version of God then?" Todd asks as he picks Jimi Hendrix's Voodoo Chile on my Spotify playlist.

"Not sure, I am single and living alone. I try to be pragmatic and not to think about it. It's almost like avoiding oneself. I seek quick pleasure to balance the pain. Drinking, snorting, streaming, sex, eating. All things that help me refrain from asking for God's help n. Each remedy applies to different stages of my life. When I was a teenager I started with pills, went on to snooze, and these days it's about booze and sex. Of course booze is more reliable and now, who knows, we can add gambling to it if all goes well. "I smile and take a look at Todd. He did not get the joke. I continue.

"I think the fundamental difference between people that ask themselves the God question and those who don't is pain and sensitivity. In my experience pain is present throughout life, according to how you were brought up. The more traumas you were exposed to, the more you are prone to suffer and search for God" I realize I am putting way too much effort in my explanation so I stop and wait for Todd to fill in the silence.

"Wow, that's a harsh way to look at it. If I think of my childhood it seems all quite boring. No big traumas. I guess I was lucky. Sometimes I'd get home and wish aliens would come down from the sky to shake things up. It all changed when I hit puberty but I would not pin it on my upbringing." r I let Todd's last statement lose steam by not replying.

"So, how do you cope when the booze doesn't work?" Todd continues.

"I go gambling. No, I am kidding. Things aren't easy. I find myself looking for a way out." I say.

"I hear you man. I have been having a real tough time at work. I have been working so hard to get promoted but it feels as if everything I do gets ignored." says Todd.

"Oh god. Work." I say.

"Sorry. I know. I shouldn't be talking about work."

"Hey, given the way I am feeling right now, I couldn't care less about work." I say. With the corner of my eye I can see Todd shift on his seat.

"What's wrong man? You know that what happens in Atlantic City, stays in Atlantic city." Todd says pulling up his sweater's sleeves. "Nothing really. I just need to get laid I guess."

When I disconnect my eye from my hearing I regain conscious focus of the road. By the side a billboard appears with huge lettering 'Family Time Matters.' Sponsored by

The Ad Council of America. The same billboard I can see from my bedroom window.

Todd is talking but the three words I have just read, Family time matters, linger in my head. I try to push them out and the word yes exits my mouth. "Yes what?" says Todd.

"Yes go on." I say. We 're never going home. We 're never going home. "Ok." Todd pauses, then carries on speaking. I am only paying attention to family, time, matters. The words have placed themselves on my windchill. I budge sideways but they remain in my frontal thinking. My mother appears. "Don't think of the white polar bear."

"What?" Todd is leaning forward with his head tilted toward me.

"Sorry man. It's a game my cousins and I would play to keep ourselves busy on long car trips. Whenever we would see a white billboard we would call it out this way. Don't ask me, it's a long story." Motherfucker. Highway lines coast the car as my thoughts roll down fucking memory lane.

I am once again back in Rome. That is in Oneida county, New York. Back in that house, looking for a reason. That's where it all started, looking outside of my window. Burgundy drapes hanging above. Out of this room, my room, I am something that doesn't work. The person I am is not wanted. I am not wanted. I am too sensitive for my mum, for the man she wants me to be t. Yes, I can still see the photos ripped out from magazines hanging on my walls. These people, Lucio Fontana, the Argentinian painter, Osho, Coco Chanel, Niels Bohr, they understand me. They know what it is like to have achieved something in life, they accept me. I am in love with the idea of making a difference, whilst outside my room it is all about 'earning a living and proving to be a real man'. This is what I mean by the impact your family has on how happy a person you will be become. It is self-realization vs calluses. There I am in my bed wondering what is wrong with me. Why don't I just want to go and help my dad knock a tree down or quit school and go to work for his mechanic friend? How can I get out of this room and face a world that just isn't my world? I look outside the window, oh yes, I remember. Then I look up at the ceiling. At the hook from where the chandelier hangs. Yes, a rope would easily slip through it.

"Check this out. I found this site where you can pick an escort and she will be at your hotel in no more than 30 minutes." Todd is proudly staring at his phone. He tries to bring it within my peripheral view but pulls it away when he either realizes that it is a hazard or that I don't really care. I pull up the collar of my shirt to cover the abrasion on the side of my neck.

"How much is it for watching?" I ask. My stomach tightens reminding me there are things that happen unbeknownst to me.

The aura of Atlantic City's lights starts to appear as our car climbs over a steep hill. As we drive closer we pass by countless motels, hotels, B&Bs. About 2 miles from the town center we pull into a First Motel on the corner of the main avenue. The sign outside advertises an offer which includes a room, breakfast and $80 worth of tokens to be spent at the Rio Grande Casino. We pull in and park in a semi-full parking lot. The quality of the entrance door reminds me of the same budget material used in my high school. Aluminum glass doors and walls built with large rectangular bricks. A red carpet on the floor leads to the reception counter.

To my delight, when we arrive no one is around, so I get to ring the bell. A man with the appearance of a minister of some Christian faith shows up behind the reception desk. I try not to focus on his looks as we are in a city where supposedly anything goes. The man is dressed as a priest and I wonder if he might be working for one of those drive-through chapels. We ask about rates, show our IDs and get our credit card swiped. Then, we walk back outside to get to our room. Imagine the typical budget motel on two floors with room access from the parking lot. We are on the second floor. When we get there we can see that the top of our Ford Focus is slightly rusting. In the room we find two twin beds with blue covers, a small round table in the corner and a bible on each of our night tables. The semi-old carpet is burgundy with thin white stripes and it spreads as far as the toilet bowl. This is what I call a room with comforts. When I'm done with unpacking I put my toiletry kit in the bathroom. As I follow the beaten path I think of all the men whose urine must have trickled down on the way back from the toilet. The quantity of it depends on the percentage of them being affected by prostatitis. Before lying on the bed, I use my index and thumb to pull the covers off.

I am suddenly reminded of the duvet cover I placed over the couch back at home. A storm of feelings I hoped I had repressed are here, alive, ready to haunt me.

Todd, having finished hanging his shirts, drags himself barefoot to the bathroom. Slight shivers travel through my back. I am staring at my reflection in the mirror above the small dresser. There is a distance between us. I see Vince but I am not that reflection.

# 12

At around 8 p.m. we set out to find a place for dinner. We leave the car in the parking lot and start strolling on the main avenue to let the neon signs entertain us. We pick a diner halfway to where the lights look really intense to avoid stupid tourist prices. I enjoy this kind of americana restaurant. You get the feeling of being in a 50's movie. The local workers sipping coffee, chatting with the waitress by the counter, the families eating cheeseburgers at round tables, and the couples savouring milkshakes in booths; but this city has nothing of that. This is the Mecca of anonymity. The good and bad of this country. It's like a clear dark sky. If you don't shine you become background.

I order a cheeseburger, Todd a BLT. Our waitress is all smiles with her sexy looks and bright make up. 30 years ago she must have been 20 and is now still wearing the same make-up colors.

"So you seeing anyone these days?" Todd asks, pushing himself to avoid the uneasiness of silence.

"Not really. There was someone I was having sex with regularly, but nothing romantic. At first we were emotionally involved but recently we seem to have finally convinced ourselves we have other priorities in life," I say.

"You find that satisfying?" Tom asks.

"I have been in a long-term relationship for 5 years. I'm now trying to make up for the time I was tied up. I think I'm only doing it because it seems easier for everyone. You know what I mean? It appears everyone is looking for 'better,' and knowing I am not 'better,' I just get what I can," I say.

"I am looking for the one. I 've tried to just date for fun but I would like to have a family soonish. You know adopt maybe, or find someone to have a baby with," Todd says as he smiles and nods his head to reinstate that he is a good guy.

"I don't think I can be with only 1 partner. Too much temptation and I've cheated before. I don't want to be weak again. The more you mature and the more you settle in your sexuality the clearer what you really want becomes," I continue as I pull the toothpick out of my mouth and suck what's on it. "I feel as though I am not really in control of my life. It's as if hormones or genes are running the show. There is an energy in me that is not allowing me to settle. For the time being, the chase is the only thing that makes me feel alive. I don't feel the need for reproduction. If you think about it, being single and having multiple partners is what man has done for most of its existence. That is our true way of being, not monogamy like we have been brainwashed to believe. 150,000 years of human evolution vs. 100 years of women's suffrage. Genes control our lives and we are just containers for these seeds. We live in order to ensure their survival. They have everything figured out. I think it's a coding that an alien race has inserted in us. Genes influence our behaviour to ensure their own survival and reproduction. I read this book, 'The Selfish Gene' by Richard Dawkins, an evolutionary biologist. He came up with a great theory which claims that humans are genes' survival machines. I actually took a photo of a page where he makes an interesting point. Let me find it, hold on." I pull my phone out, scroll through the images I have saved and find the article with the quote.

- Genes are usually packed together inside a genome, which is itself contained inside an organism, or a human being. They build vehicles (bodies) to promote their mutual interests of jumping into the next generation of vehicles. -

Todd nods and says. "That's a good metaphor. Vehicles. Would the two of us be 'damaged vehicles' then? If we don't have kids we are going against the master plan.

Well, I am planning to have children soon." Todd comments, holding his phone in his hand.

Todd has blue eyes, dry blonde hair, and a goatee. He is nothing special but definitely a catch for an Asian woman looking to reinforce her Americanness. "You know what's the most interesting part of the book? The idea that we are altruistic not because of our upbringing or religious belief but because our gene view others as additional vehicles that need to be safeguarded for overall gene survival. I laughed when I first read it. I thought Jesus, Saint Francis, Mother Theresa and I have something in common. We don't have children. These people gave up their lives to ensure that others would survive. Maybe this is where my genes are leading me to." I say as Todd takes a big sip of his root beer.

"Well by looking around, there is definitely a lot of work for holy men," says Todd as to wrap the whole conversation up. He pauses for about 5 seconds and continues "We are probably still too immature to have kids. That's all.

Wouldn't want you to come to work wearing a tunic and with the top of your head shaved."

The waitress, wearing a short-sleeved white cotton dress comes over with two big round plates. When I stop to think whether what I said to Todd makes any sense, I notice that a guy at the booth next to ours is staring at me. I look away, but from the corner of my eye I see that he keeps on looking. After a couple of minutes I decide to speak.

"How you doing?" I ask as I am about to bite my burger. I get self-conscious when people look at me while I'm eating.

"I'm fine, man. It's you I'm worried about," the man says. He has a shiny bald head, an Anton Van Dyck goatee with a clean-shaven space between his chin and moustache, and a scarification of Greek letters on his lower right bicep, Alpha Phi Alpha. Looks like he has just been pumping. I lean back to descry what shoes he is wearing. White Adidas Stan Smith Primeknit.

"Is there too much artery-clogging fat in my burger?" I ask. The man smiles at my comeback but quickly reverses to his frown.

"I've been watching you since you sat down. I couldn't miss how tense you are. By the way I am Byron," he says as he extends his hand. He applies the right pressure. Enough to keep the connection lingering without being intrusive.

"You mean my calorie consumption is over the recommended 1500 daily intake?" I say.

"No man, it's simple, you just don't breathe," Byron says.

"You saying I'm a zombie or something? I don't breathe?" I try to focus on my breathing but it feels like taking off training wheels. It comes natural until you pay attention to it.

"You take these short little breaths that will end up asphyxiating you," he says as he slides closer to us.

"True. Actually, I'm practicing for when I give birth." I say. "When was the last time you took a proper deep breath?" The fraternity man says.

"Last time I did coke? No. Seriously. I don't know. Do you know of anyone who pays attention to their breaths?" I ask.

"We get caught up in all sort of things but forget the most basic thing that allows us to do it all. I used to be like you, but when I got really sick I was taught that to get back into things I had to start from the most basic actions."

"Like breathing?" I hide a deep breath through my nostrils.

"Right on," he says as he watches my diaphragm enlarge.

Byron was a fairly bright kid who had gotten into a good college to become a doctor. While at university he tried out for the baseball team and with great surprise to his parents, made the team. Of course, being in a varsity team turned those 4 college years into a blur, leaving him little time for books. He soon found himself failing classes and having to change majors from medicine to liberal arts. After graduating it seemed a natural step to get into pro-ball, but that proved to be a disappointment as a result of a cartilage injury. He fell into depression and after a suicide attempt his family checked him into a rehab clinic. There, he had to choose between letting the stigma of mental illness become himself or use his experience as a tool to help others.

"So how do you feel these days?" I ask, anxious to find in his answer something that could help me with my own emotional turbulence.

"It was a nice 'vacation,' that's how I like to refer to it. I read an interesting book called Ecce by this guy Frank Doorty which I recommend you read. He talks of his own enlightenment and of how before reaching it he attempted suicide and ended up on the streets. Essentially the philosophy he came up with is that only by concentrating on the now you can escape the sadness of the past and the stress deriving from the unpredictability of the future. Being in the now is possible by becoming aware of your thoughts and emotions and not going along with them. So, the simple revelation is that you are not thoughts. By concentrating on your breathing, you start to realize that you are not your thoughts, but rather awareness. It's a bit like being aware that you are watching a movie instead of losing yourself in it. Thoughts create ideals of how things should be, but we should really learn to just "be." If we do that, we stop setting expectations and consequently stop being deceived, which means no longer becoming unhappy. Remember we are human beings not human doings. " says the bald man.

"Whooo. Sounds easy. I have tried meditation to be more in control of my thoughts but I have always ended up falling asleep," I say.

"Like everything that is good for us, it takes time and patience. What is good for the mind is hard for the body and what is good for the body is hard for the mind." Byron says.

Byron's statement leaves me perplexed and in order not to look lost I ask: "So what are you doing here, anyway? This does not seem like the place for someone who's figured out that life runs on breaths."

"I'm here for a conference but I never miss a chance to share what I know with a handsome man like yourself," says Byron.

I raise my eyebrows as I am still digesting his statement about mind and body. Todd quietly sneaks away to go to the toilet while Byron goes on.

"You know man, I find most people have made their working career what they identify with and the reason why the wake up every morning. This reason is called "status." Jean-Paul Sartre, a French philosopher, said: 'We are social animals. Hell is other people.' So people spend a lifetime to ensure their status and surround themselves by others who can reflect it. But then look at individuals who have had a real impact on humanity like Buddha, St. Francis, Gandhi. They were all people who had status and gave it up for the good of everyone. They figured that the real challenge was not to make yourself happy but to make everyone happy. They just brought it to a whole other level. You dig?" Byron's eyes are dark with a slightly yellow sclera. He reaches in his pocket and extracts a business card.

Byron John Lloyd

Mindfulness Coach

Health & Mind College Certified

053 366 4893 B.Now@HM.com

To be polite, I take the time to glare over it.

"So who are your clients? I mean, what type of problems do you deal with?" I ask.

"It depends. I freelance at retreats and alternative medicine centers that are affiliated with the institution I belong to." Byron says.

"I might give you a call if I decide to go on a retreat then," I say as I look at the card again.

"You do that and remember. Breathe. It's the only freedom left to us." He gets up, lays the cash to pay his bill on the table and leaves.

# 13

Throughout my entire conversation with Byron, Todd did not utter a single word. It is actually something I admire in him as he seemingly doesn't need to always make his point. To me being a good listener is a trait of confidence, an armor against other people's invisible ego-arrows, more simply known as judgments. He never complains, he is humorous, he believes in his work and he has only one real vice that I know of. Thinking about it, I realize I am little envious of Todd. Probably because I see how easily he fits in, how easily he flows with life. Or at least this is my perception of him. We pay the check and as I breathe in Byron's empiricism I try to digest all that my Robin Hood therapist has handed me.

Todd and I walk side by side on a pristine sidewalk. It feels good to put to use what was built only to respect an urban engineer's plan. As we stroll down the street we both seem fascinated by the city lights' potency devoid of great tall buildings. We pass by what must be one of the first casinos built in the city. Rio Grande. The beginning, the frontier of what used to be just a dream and turned out to be a reality. Like a boxer who is past his prime, the building is imposing with its width and height but stands stiff with its shapeless architecture and lack of bright energy. The furnishings inside do not match the date on the plaque outside celebrating its 1964 opening. A series of Erte's paintings hang at a perfect distance from one another in the hall.

Glass walls divide the bar from the blackjack tables and the jackpot machines.

As we take a seat at the bar to get adjusted to the geriatric euphoria, we scan the environment to understand how to wrestle our fortune.

I look at Todd and ask him: "Does everyone here think they have a chance?" He is leaning forward on the counter, sucking on a straw in his Moscow Mule as he looks straight ahead.

"What do you mean? A chance for the better?" Todd lets the straw drop into his drink.

"I'm just thinking about the people that come here. You know what I mean? Why do you become a gambler?" I say. Todd keeps his lips tight and moves them right and left. Maybe he finds me a bit heavy going with all these philosophical questions.

"I think it's fascinating. Try shutting your eyes and listen to the sounds". Todd says smiling as he slowly slides off his stool. He tells me he will go check out the blackjack table.

I decide for a more passive engagement. I find old ladies in elastic-waist pants sitting tensely in front of rows of slot machines. I stop three quarters of the way in an aisle where sounds and lights fight each other to get my coins. Not having played before, I stop by what seems remotely familiar, a slot machine with fruit icons. I stare at the machine hoping to understand what I'm supposed to do and when I look to my left it all becomes clear. I decide to copy every move the Filipina woman next to me is doing. When she digs into her coin bucket, I place my hand in mine, pull out a coin and slowly direct it toward the coin drop. Her outstretched arm shows the flesh hanging over her triceps which dangles when she reaches for the lever. We simultaneously push the lever down and as I see the images spin I look over her machine to check whose fruits are rolling faster. When they begin to slow down, I quickly try to read the game rules written on the corner of the glass screen. When the images stop rolling, I see grapes, a strawberry, and a banana. As I wait to find out whether I have won I hear the sound of coins pouring from my friend's machine. She picks them up mechanically, without excitement, and pours them back into the bucket. I look at her feeling my facial expression transitioning from surprise to disappointment. An impulse I don't recognise fights its way into my consciousness. I imagine myself walking slowly behind the woman, raising my coin bucket to hit her over the head. I do this repeatedly until I see thick red blood flow over the machine dashboard.

Unsettled by this emotion, I quickly get off my stool and leave the cup of coins. I walk away pulling the zipper of my jacket up. A burning sensation awakens in the pit of my stomach and reaches the area just below my thorax. I imagine a round flesh opening, the ripping of stomach muscles being eaten away by a lake of dissolving acid. When I walk over to Todd to tell him I need to get out, my heart is pounding, making it hard to breathe. Gastric acid is climbing up my throat burning everything on its path. I don't give Tom the time to question. I rush outside trying to breathe in the warm, solid air. I spit out what I can and think of Byron whilst I take a fucking deep breath. Vince concentrate only on the sensation of the air filling up the lungs and then slowly, automatically, exiting through the nostrils. When my eyes meet the pavement, Danielle's blood spreads beneath my shoes. I pull my head up, take another deep breath and find a church's billboard right across the street that says: "Mother Mary loved you this much." Mother Mary' arms are spread on the cross and blood trickles profusely from her hands and feet. I flag down a cabbie and text Todd asking him to meet me directly back at the motel. Once in the car, I turn around to look back at the holy sign and behind it, over towering it another billboard reads 'Family Time Matters' sponsored by The Ad Council of America.

"Hey, it's Vince." When I dial Melissa's number I am lying on the bed face down, legs crossed and with my ingrown pinky toenail scraping the top of the bed's foot board.

"Heeeey Vince! What a surprise. What are you up to?" Melissa makes me feel like she cares.

"I'm in Atlantic City with a friend." I want to say more to hide my tension, but I can't.

"I didn't make you out to be the card-playing type." She says. "Me neither, but I thought I should give it a try. Take a chance on destiny, or I should say I was hoping destiny would take a chance on me." "Oh c'mon I am sure you have taken a chance on me. So what are you doing tonight? "

"Not sure yet. We haven't decided."

"You should go to this club called Foldam. I went there after a conference and it was quite interesting. I think you would enjoy it. When will you be back? If you really want to do something different, I got something for you. Let's meet up when you get back," Melissa says, raising my hopes really high.

I did a bit of searching online and it seems like Foldam club is a good choice. I was looking for a place with a local feel, good music and good gay/straight ratio. I guess Melissa and I have more and more in common. The entrance is made of a small wooden door overshadowed by a black reclining canape.

There is a street light about 20 feet away whose shade circumference just about reaches Coco's black Air Jordan III OG. That is the name by which those on the list greet the biggest black man I have ever seen up close. His neck is one with his shoulders and his arms stand distant upheld by his lats. The skin at the base of his neck overflows in two fleshy rolls. Over them growths of small ingrown hairs light up a desire too pleasurable to suppress. Passing a wood plane over the base of his neck to guillotine the protruding warts. Now, that is satisfaction.

Coco is wearing a black suit, a black shirt and a black tie. The skin on his face is thick, blotched by age. His expression is the petrified version of the moment in which he failed the tryouts for the Jacksonville Jaguars. It comes alive when someone skips the line and approaches the velvet rope with a money shake.

The dance floor is unlit. Dim lights on its sides direct you to the bar. We walk up to the counter on the right of the dance floor to ease in the atmosphere. It's Todd's turn to buy drinks.

I stand by the side of the bar taking in what I can, which is limited. The faces I can discern are darkened by concentration and narcosis. The vibrations are potent. No sign of fucking around here. No flirting, grinding or posing. My aggression fades with each beat. I welcome the beats as gentle caresses. As the RPM increase I can feel their vibration on my lower back and behind my ears. I start nodding my head to invite them to continue. As the bass line morphs from deep to deeper I stretch my neck sideways to show it acceptance and trust. When the rhythm turns into throbbing I feel it chest bump me and I let my back arch to allow for the rhythm to flow through me. When the acutes drop like stalactites, I want them to penetrate me from my throat down to my anus. I follow the beat like a predator. I notice a crew cut, soft nose, light skin, perforated by a cheek piercing. I get closer. With a faster tempo it lifts its head. I see a light shimmering from a damp neck. I want to bite it, lick it. Drink from it.

Todd comes over, hands me a drink and tells me he is moving to the other room. I follow him. The atmosphere feels softer. Anger hides in the dark corners. I reach for my pocket and swallow an ecstasy pill with my vodka Redbull. Then, I go sit on a couch and watch Todd approaching the border of the dance floor as he slightly bops his head. I wait. Wait for the MDMA to improve me. I want to smile. So I let myself. I stretch my legs and recline. I am so utterly alone. But here everyone seems to have come for that very same reason. They don't know it or don't want to admit it, but the music is an angel liberating us from others. The bar light expands and retracts mimicking my eye movement. Yes, yes, the beat is the thrust of a missile spiking into euphoria.

I get up. I need to move to sanctify this harmony.

I open my eyes and it is by me. I close my eyes again and I feel its smell. I see its neck. The glistening of the skin like a smooth granite wall. My chemical heat is different to the one approaching. Inside, an incinerator burns along with my feelings and thoughts. I am fire. I need those sweat drops to fall on me.

When I leave the toilet stall, my back arches and twists to adjust to the room temperature. The heat is still inside between the wooden walls. On my way out, I stop and seek the mirror.

My , my, is this what we are made of.

I wet my hands and pull my face back.

# 14

Next day, on our way back, Todd tries to chit chat. Black Ray Ban are not enough to dim the triviality of life. So clear, so everywhere. It's in my face and yet it is so distant from all my brain believes in.

Melissa. Her hair is so blond I would categorize it as exotic. I usually use this adjective to describe non-western women, but I now realize it includes any trait that is at the extreme on the human feature scale. In basic terms, if her pubic hair is different from mine, I find it exotic. Melissa is wearing knee high black boots, a denim skirt to her knees, black tights, and a leather jacket. When we meet up at the entrance of Getty Park, we embrace like longtime friends and start walking down the gravel path towards the lake. After preliminary talk on how we are, Melissa tells me about her night out and hints of a man she seems to be interested in. I mull this over, her voice in the background. We sit on a bench. My heart is still standing.

"So how was the trip?" she asks quietly.

"Cool. Didn't get much betting done. Met some strange, entertaining people, but I don't think it's my type of vacation." I say.

"I had a great time when I went. Did you go to the Foldam Bar? I loved that place!" Melissa says.

"Yes, we did. We got hammered, and I can't really remember much." I laugh abruptly. "I needed a break. B I have been having a bit of a hard time lately."

"Really? What's up?" Melissa, sitting next to me, leans forward and slightly sideways to look at my face.

"Mmmm. I am not sure as how to put it. It's not something I have had happen to me before." I say.

"Well, try me. I thought we were friends." It's amusing how such a beautiful word can sometimes acquire a completely opposite meaning when you are in love.

"I saw a woman die." Only after I said it I think of how heavy those words must sound. Putting my needs first, I 'll take all a friend can offer.

"Oh, God! When? Who?" Melissa quickly tenses up and pushes her head further toward me.

"About a week ago. I didn't know her. I never saw someone die before. I mean, I didn't see her die. First she was alive and then I woke up and saw her dead."

"What do you mean 'first she was alive, and then she was dead'?" Melissa asks.

My thoughts are racing, and my hands are getting sweaty.

"I mean I believe that after talking to me she jumped off my balcony," I say, watching a duck plunge into the water. Only the back end and legs stick out.

"What did you say to her?"

"Me? Nothing. She was going to tell me something, but obviously didn't." I suddenly realise that to Melissa, or to anyone else for that matter, this might all sound pretty fucking confusing.

"Did you know her? How did she get into your house?" Melissa asks. "I know it sounds unbelievable, but I let her in. She was running from someone, and supposedly I also should have been running from the same people she was running from. Since she seemed to know who I was I thought I should find out more by inviting her to my place. Yes I am that fucking gullible." Talking about it is not actually helping. Despite myself, a sense of dissociation kicks in. I feel as I am being squeezed out of myself.

"Have you told the police? It wasn't your fault! Right?" Says Melissa. "Well, I really had nothing to do with it, and I don't want to be involved in it. I have no alibi, and

I've seen a friend get into lots of trouble for being an eyewitness to a hit-and-run," I say.

"How do you feel now?"

"It's ok when I am surrounded by people and I am doing something. As soon as I am alone though, I get flashbacks about her."

"I think I might have something that can help you."

"What? A mind-eraser gadget like the one in that Jim Carry movie, Eternal Sunshine of the Spotless Mind?"

"No, you dummy. If you want, I can hook you up with some interesting girls who downloaded the app I am working on. It's a great way to do something healthy and to shut your mind off. Best medicine around, don't you think? That is if you are into women only..." Melissa says, resting her hand on my knee.

"I have to admit I have not been intimate with a woman for a while, and it could definitely help me put things into perspective. I don't know what to say... Thanks."

"You don't have to say anything. Just take it as a present from a friend." "You never told me how you got into this project." I say.

"I want to become a behavioral psychologist and specialise in sexual disorders caused by digital media. So I joined a small startup to launch the app I told you about. I can basically make your profile appear as much as possible, give you 5 stars on your member reviews so that we can easily find you the hottest girls," Melissa says smiling.

As if I were looking through a spyglass, my emotions, my thoughts, all things around me, feel so far away. Only my skin feels tight and raw. I can sense my synapses spark like a severed electrical cable. They send sparks into my head as it rotates on itself like in the Exorcist movie. I cross my arms and bend forward to hold myself.

"All you need to do is open a profile. I will find you the best candidates and let you know. Only thing you can do for me is to write an encounter review when you get the user feedback email," Melissa continues.

"So you already have lots of members?" I ask.

"Yes. I thought it would be quite hard, but then we got a couple of positive reviews from TechCrunch and Wired magazine. What really made it happen was a short article from Cosmo.com. Members are quite discrete and this is why I thought it could be a good way to get you out of your rut. If you want, I can make those tweaks on your profile and see the results we get," Melissa says.

"Yes. I need something to take me out of my head. I will be a proper study participant and make a proper report. I promise." I give her the best fake smile I can manage.

# 15

Jasmine is my ex-girlfriend. I dated her on and off for 3 years. I'm not sure what I would say if someone asked me why it didn't work out between us. Maybe because she's made me realize I pay way too much attention to a woman's body. Its shape makes it a visceral attraction. Our relationship, after dating, went to about 3 years of occasional sex to finally morph into friendship. We love each other and have accepted we can't be together more than a day at a time.

Jasmine and I are experiencing the latest relationship evolution between man and woman. Women can now be there for a man, support him, advise him, offer all the noble characteristics of friendship and add physical pleasure to it all.

My mother keeps asking me when I will settle down. In my life I have only met a couple of women I have found interesting as people, sex aside. To be objective, and by that I mean my honest point of view, I find women to be overall quite purposeful but not interesting for a lifetime, not in the same way a man can be. I tell my mother I would love to be with someone but I just can't stand the emotional rollercoaster. And I don't mean theirs but mine. For a long time I have been trying to understand why I end up with partners I don't trust and consequently become jealous of. My therapist believes I have unresolved trust issues with my mother and am therefore unable to open up.

"So which one do you think works best?" Jasmine holds the pipes in her hand. I am not sure why she asked me to accompany her to the hardware store since she probably knows more than I do about these things. Her hands are short but elongated by artificial nails. I think the way they are painted is what is called a Reverse French manicure. You highlight the white semi-circle at the base of the nail. Big brown eyes, Mediterranean curls with blond highlights, straight roman nose, and a cleft above her lips; but what I love most is her thirty five-year-old tanned skin. There comes a time when you prefer worn over new.

Old shoes over new ones, old wallet over a new one, anal over vaginal.

"The plumber told me I need to get five 40 inches pipes of this diameter," she says as her thumb and index try to circumvent the girth.

"Vince, can you go and look for help?" Jasmine says, looking at me the way she did the first time we met. Through me.

As I walk down the aisle I tell myself 'Yes, I do need help.' Then I think "this is why we are no longer together." I don't like to be bossed around. Why is it that I attract bossy women? Once again my therapist view is that I am looking for those that are similar to my mother.

After a couple of aisles I return and find her talking to a floor assistant.

"Hold this." She loads 5 pipes onto my curled arms.

"Ron promised he would do all of this for me. He started the job and now my bathroom looks like Ground Zero."

"Are you still talking to him?" I ask as I see those cute stumpy hands grab the cold pipes from my arms and drop them on the register counter.

"I hate him." Her head is low and I can see her plentiful breasts from her low hanging blouse.

"He seemed to care about you." I say.

"Maybe. But he wasn't there when I tested him."

"Did he know that he was being tested?" I ask.

"Whatever. I was always ready to please him whenever he needed it. I just want to be loved. Does that have to be so hard?!" She pushes her credit card into her Chloe pocketbook.

"I know, but we don't all think the same way and a man needs to be guided into what a woman wants. Slowly. Really slowly." I say.

"I don't have time for this bullshit. I need someone who knows what he wants." Jasmine says as she signs the credit card slip.

The granola bars by the check-out aisle awaken my stomach.

"Do you want to eat something? I need some sugar in my blood." I ask quietly. Sugar helps me keep bad thoughts away.

"Where do you want to go?" She lays her right hand on my thigh. She then puts lipstick on and starts the car.

"We could order a takeaway."

# 16

---

The city's conference center is on my way to work. This week's event is 'Regression Therapy - Annual Conference 2015.'

There is a huge banner in front of the building with the conference's name on it. Above the letters is an image of the sun on the horizon and a silhouette of a person walking on a beach. As my eyes wander back from the banner to the sidewalk, a group of people wearing name tags around their necks flow out in front of me. Before they take over the sidewalk, I speed up my pace to get around them. As I am about to take over the head of the herd, I feel someone grab my shoulder. I turn around and see a familiar face I can't place.

"Hey." I don't say more, as I don't remember the person's name. "Byron Lloyd Johnson is the name you are looking for. What, you threw my card away?" he says smiling.

"Oh, yeah, Atlantic City, right? What you doing here?" I ask, looking at the badge hanging from his neck.

"I'm here for this conference." Byron raises his eyes toward the banner.

"I was actually looking at the banner and wondering what it is about." I put my hands in my pockets.

"By the looks of the banner, I would say it is about tourism for the senile," Byron says. "It's about regression hypnosis. Do you know about it?" His face is round and hairless, like that of a child. It reminds me of a documentary on the theory of beauty which claims that what creates mutual sexual attraction is a perfectly even skull structure. It seems that, like with emotions, balance is what we are after.

"Has it to do with going back to your childhood to find out what is wrong in your adult life?" I see the air condense as my breath ushers the words.

"Close, but it goes further. People get hypnotized to regress into their past lives." Byron speaks slowly and pronounces each word clearly. I'd like to know more, but the cold makes the tips of my fingers tingle and my temple starts to hurt.

"I have to run, but why don't we meet up for a coffee later?" I say. "Yeah, sure. I am usually done after 5," Byron says as he checks his Tag Heur's Carrera.

I ask Melissa to come and meet Byron. I think they might get along. What they do is somewhat related. I am not sure why I expose a woman I am interested into another man. I am a sucker for good causes. I am the good cause.

We meet at a tea house. We choose a table by the corner, set against the wall. On the opposite side a large window looks out onto the sidewalk.

Before sitting down, I get a sense of Déjà vu. It's so intense that to snap out of it, it takes Melissa pulling me down to the chair. Melissa and Byron are both staring at me and I smile to put them back at ease. Melissa is looking rather pale in her red North Face fleece matched with a white t-shirt underneath. When I am able to focus again, I explain to Byron how I met Melissa.

"I met Melissa kind of like how I met you. Unexpectedly." I explain the whole cold-calling thing.

"This is what makes my life worth living. What I can't expect," says Melissa.

"We are all part of a bigger scheme." I say.

"In what way?" asks Byron as he leans backward and looks at me. I look at Melissa in return, as if the answer should come from her.

She smiles, showing her beautiful teeth and lets the conversation die.

"So what do you do Melissa?" Byron skillfully changes topic.

"I am training to be a behavioral psychologist," Melissa replies. She goes on turning into her professional persona which I had yet to meet. "I am researching the role and impact of digital media on sexual behavior." Melissa continues.

"Sex is no longer a 2-person thing," says Byron.

"Yes, with AIDS, technology, and women's independence through the pill, we have developed a more self-sufficient behavior towards sexuality," says Melissa.

"As a woman do you feel the web has further emancipated women sexually?" Byron asks.

"What do you mean?" Melissa says lifting her elbows on the table and resting her head on her clenched hands.

"Do you think you got into this sort of research because of the way you experience sex? Sounds a bit voyeuristic," says Byron.

"I am not sure I understand what you mean by that," says Melissa. Ying stops flowing into yang, but they do smile at each other for what feels like an eternity.

Melissa continues. "Well the web is pretty much a way to experience without really being there. That is the advantage and the disadvantage of it."

"Byron, what exactly are you doing at this conference?" I say, pulling my chair as close as possible to the table, re-creating a neutral space.

"We are discussing the best hypnosis techniques. We use them to get people to regress into their past lives and find out what happened that still has an impact on their current life."

"Such as?" I ask.

"Let's say someone is suffering from chronic neck pain and does not seem to find a cure for it. Through past life regression, we can discover if being stabbed in the neck in a former life, for instance, causes this pain. By going back and having the patient face it, which means becoming conscious of it, we unlock the energy that makes the pain chronic. We unlock an emotional bottleneck," Byron explains.

"So what happens when you do this?" I say as I imagine myself mumbling on a couch half asleep.

"It's not like going to the dentist. As a patient you need to be involved in the process. I mean, you need to willingly let your mind's guard down. Some people don't like not being in control." Byron takes a sip of his tea to lubricate his explanation, but Melissa beats him to it and presents me with her own version of the explanation.

"There are 3 steps. The first phase is to regress and find the root of the problem. The second phase is for the patient to project his present self into the past life and personality. The third phase is to accept what has been experienced and come to terms with the past trauma in order to move on and shed its negative hold on the present life." Melissa recites each word as if reading out of a manual.

"Well done. Yes, it's that simple Vince," says Byron, giving me a fake smile. The toothless kind.

"The head of my department circulated a study on it last year." Melissa explains how she is so well versed on the topic.

"A woman with many hidden talents," Byron comments. "Hey Vince, you should come to the conference tomorrow. Who knows, you might find regression hypnosis so interesting that you'll join a workshop on it I will give next month."

Once the waiter comes over we order a tea with biscuits and start talking about what else Byron could do while in town.

# 17

The following day I email Melissa to check if she has been able to find any good matches in her database. She tells me that her team is working on the algorithm and that in a couple of hours the profile matches will start coming in. I am feeling more nervous than I thought I would be and it surprises me. It's not about the sex. It's about meeting someone I've never seen before in a cold turkey sort of way.

Today is Byron's last day at the conference. I've declined his invitation. I have been summoned by my boss to discuss my performance at work. Byron is in the main auditorium, taking a break before the last presentation. He is going through his notes. He instinctively lifts his head, glances at the people coming in and goes right back to his notes. As he searches through his papers and pamphlets, an image hacks his attention. He looks up again and realizes that it's her, moving between rows 1 and 2. Melissa. As he stares at the thick blond hair he wonders if her attendance is due to the discussion they've had or if it is related to her own research. He looks at his watch, realizes he still has time before the next session and decides to walk down and say hi.

"Hey, what are you doing here?" Byron leans forward to shrink his imposing body.

"Hey! Called a school friend last night and got hold of a ticket," Melissa says as she moves her bag to let Byron sit down.

"Have you been here since this morning? Interesting stuff, don't you think?" says Byron.

"Yes, very. Is this a therapeutic procedure you use, or is it just an interest?" Melissa asks.

"No, I've never used it, but I really want to start training in it." Says Byron.

"If you are interested, I might know someone at my research center that could help. Let's exchange numbers before you leave so I can text you his name." Melissa adjusts herself on the seat to pull up her skirt. The day's main event, Healing Mental Illness through Past Life Regression Hypnosis' begins with a presentation given by the president of Melissa's institute.

Dr. Bauer gets on stage silently. For about 30 seconds the audience struggles to understand if he is the main speaker or a technician. He is a small, thin man, in his sixties, with a strong distinguishing feature. A blood spot, the circumference of a coke can, on his forehead. Just like former Russian president Mikhail Gorbachev.

"Ladies and gentlemen, glad you could make it today. I know it will be challenging to go back in time a few hundred years when in the age of social media everything needs to happen in real time. Bear with me and restrain that finger." Dr. Bauer continues his presentation giving some background on the topic.

"In ancient Indian literature, there are different sources where past-life regression is mentioned such as the Upanishads and the Yoga Sutras of Patañjali. On this latter source the Hindu scholar Patañjali talks of the soul becoming burdened with an accumulation of impressions as part of the karma from previous lives.[4] In China a deity called the "Lady of Forgetfulness" prevented souls from remembering their past lives with a potion to erase all memories before reincarnating.

In the modern era, past life regression therapy has been studied since the 1950s by psychologists, psychiatrists and mediums. It wasn't until 1988, that this topic gained mainstream recognition when Todd Weiss, an American psychiatrist and a Yale graduate, published best-selling Many Lives, Many Masters.

So after this short intro on the topic, let me tell you about my research. In my own practice I have found that

Past Life Regression has proved to be successful when dealing with issues whose origin or cause is unclear, especially in pathologies such as chronic anxiety and depression.

We are familiar with the ancient Latin expression "Mens sana in Corpere sano" by Roman poet Juvenal. A sound mind in a sound body. The correlation of mind and body and their interdependence has been widely recognised. As we can infer from the great success of the Yoga practice, the masses are awakening to this millennial truth. We quiet the mind by focusing on the body. In Regression Hypnosis we have discovered that an unhealthy mind can originate from a physical trauma that occurred in a past life.

Let me present the case of Stephanie in support of this finding. The client was experiencing loss of consciousness, trouble sleeping, and most importantly severe depression. We performed blood tests to check whether her thyroid is functioning properly, and MRIs to check the state of brain neural circuitry in all areas of the brain. The test results were all negative. During her regression, it emerged she was raped and violently killed in an 18th century Russian castle. After being confronted with this finding during a therapeutic session, I recorded a decrease in her mood swings." Dr. Bauer goes on explaining how this technique can be usefully applied to severely mentally ill patients.

He presents additional slides on trial patients supporting his research and results. At the end of the presentation, Byron looks around and spots Melissa checking her mobile. He slowly closes his Mac caressing the top cover. The softness of his hand grinds to halt when it reaches the plastic of the Apple logo. Melissa untangles her hair and runs her fingers through them. Byron approaches her and asks if she is free for a drink and if she would like to discuss past life regression further.

# 18

Ginger is my first profile match and I am meeting her at a bowling alley. Judging from her profile photo she is undoubtedly stunning but the gesture she is making gets me wandering. I have seen some girl friends on Facebook do it, tongue sticking out whilst making the sign V with the index and middle finger. My dyke friend Jenny told me it is a part-time lesbian code for 'I am into cunninglingus.'

Melissa seems very confident in the fact that Ginger and I will be a good match, since she reviewed our profiles and 'manipulated' the match.

I am to walk to the counter and ask for the lane reserved under her name. "Number 8," says the girl at the desk. I walk down the lanes and I see different strokes for different folks. As I approach Ginger's lane, my ears are filled with the vibrations of a strike and the fulfilling sound it creates. I don't know of another sport where the same visual and audio combination exists.

My lady is wearing an Adidas track top and skinny jeans. Her thick red hair goes down to her shoulders. Her nose is pointy and adorned by some light freckles. Her eyes are wide and green and her nails are painted with transparent polish. Picking up the bowling balls will certainly discern a real manicure from a fake one. When I approach her to shake her hand she turns around holding the ball, which causes me to awkwardly pull my hand away.

I lean my upper body forward to hug her but abort my attempt when she stands still, protected by the ball. She smiles and tells me she will be right back. She goes for a throw. As she stands in concentration before releasing the ball, I stare at her skinny legs tightly aligned one against the other. They are slightly curved; I distinguish a tiny wedge in between. Her buttocks are small, tense and round. In between flat and plump. She takes the steps to release the ball and as she leans forward to ease the ball on the lane, her jacket lifts up revealing a fuchsia string. She is cordial but distant and as we exchange formalities a small muscle spasm appears right below her right eye. Two thoughts are crossing my mind. First, there's gotta be something wrong for a woman to want to meet a man this way. Second, there is nothing wrong with me, so there can't be anything wrong with her.

We go through the motions of speed courting, wearing our masks or shields depending on how you view it. A mask if you prefer to hide. A shield if you want no holds barred. We know too well there is someone else behind our covers and that is why we have chosen to meet through a mobile app. We both have a desperate need to forgo all the protection. Just two people looking for quick honesty.

"How long have you been on AppYours?" Ginger asks.

"Not very long, a couple of weeks. And you?" I say as I wait for her reaction.

"I would say about 10 days. My friends told me to join as I have just come out of a bad relationship. So a little fun won't hurt." Ginger says as her top lip curls up. "Have you been out with someone already?" She asks.

Yes a couple of times. How about you?" I ask.

"Yes sure. A few times." Says Ginger. I blush inside.

"You play often? I mean bowling."

"I used to when I was at Uni. Helps me unwind. You want to go for a throw?" She says.

"Sure."

We continue talking as we alternate throws. She tells me she is a counsellor for a charity that works with teenagers.

"So you studied psychology?" I ask as I grab my beer.

"Yes at uni and then I did a master in psychotherapy." Says Ginger, as she has also come over the small table behind the bowling lane.

"I got a question for you. I have a friend who's read this book by Carl Jung. I think it's called "Man and his Symbols". It kind of changed his life. I wish I came across a book that changed my life. Actually there is one, but it probably made my life worse."

"Oh, what is it?" She asks.

"Freud's Interpretations of Dreams." I answer with a dumb smile.

"Yes, that is a groundbreaking book. I would have to say the two books are like love and war." She says as she sits, crosses her legs and tucks her right foot behind her left calf.

"Well what do you think of Jung?" I ask.

"He is great. He came up with this brilliant theory about archetypes. Symbolic figures we all share within our dreams."

"What kind of symbols?"

"Well one of them is the divine child, for instance. It represents our true self, the wholeness of our being. In dreams the Divine Child may bear the semblance of a baby or infant. It is both defenseless yet inviolate. It is the archetype of the totality of our being, the regenerative energy that with the power of transformation directs us toward wholeness Then there is the Anima, a symbolic figure for the female part of your personality. For example, you could dream of being dressed up as woman for example. The Shadow is the archetype which embodies the aspects of yourself that you have repressed or never recognized, that you reject and don't want others to see. The Shadow is generally regarded as a symbol of weakness, fear and anger, which in a dream might be represented by a stalker or by a murder.

Jung believed that everyone shares these sort of symbols in their dreams as we all share one unconscious, the collective unconscious." Ginger explains. "I recently had a dream in which I was following someone." I admit . Then I look down, realising that Ginger might find my confession rather creepy. She smiles and keeps going.

"Talking about Jung and Freud actually reminds me of an interesting story I've heard when I was interning at St Andrew's hospital. So Jung and Freud were great buddies. Just like you and the friend you mentioned." She slightly nudges me with her elbow, then continues. "They loved each other's theories so much that on their first meeting they spent 13 hours together. After a few years though, according to the official version, t they broke up over a disagreement on the degree of influence sexuality has in human motivation. Freud, unlike Jung, thought it was absolute.

Some speculate that Jung suffered a 6 years mental break down because of the separation from Freud. Some say that the breakdown was due to his repressed homosexual attraction towards Freud. "She opens her eyes wide, as if inviting me to read her mind.

"Wow. Who would have known?" I say, as I think of the ways in which Zac and I differ, the dichotomy reflected in our respective book's choice. Zac, impacted by Jung. Me, by Freud. I quickly ask Ginger if she wants to go for one more game. "

Ginger smiles, gets up and tells me she'd like to teach me an easy bowling technique. She stands behind me. I can feel her breast push against my back. As I bring the ball in front of me with my right hand, she places hers on my throwing wrist. She follows as I bring back my arm and when I extend it forward she tells me when to release.

We go on for about 7 games and as we finish our beers she asks me if we should go. I agree and follow her.

When I walk into her apartment, I search for clues of her everyday life since I believe that where you live shows who you are inside. Everything is so neat, no books, no photos or paintings. I wonder if she AirBnB'd the place. I want to ask her if she just moved in but I'd rather not get too personal. I stick to ceremonials telling her what a nice place it is. She invites me to sit on the couch and offers me a drink. I look forward to it to ease the tension. Funny how since what happened with Danielle alcohol has established itself in my life and how I am encountering it much more often than I used to.

I follow the sound she makes while she is in the kitchen pouring wine. Then a few moments of silence is go by. The silence is replaced by approaching footsteps. My gaze is lost on the switched off flat screen. The sound of her movements is so soothing that I can feel it move through my ear canal and slide on my skin. Then, it turns into a déjà vu I can't place. When she reappears she is wearing a rust colored silk robe that matches her hair color perfectly. I tense up and slowly readjust myself on the couch. She places our drinks on a glass table in front of the couch and sits next to me. As she leans forward to grab the drinks, her perfume penetrates my nostrils. She reclines back and her robe opens slightly showing her cleavage.

The silk lets her slide easily on the leather couch as she gathers her legs sideways. Her flip-flops fall on the floor. She is defenseless with both hands occupied by the wine glasses whose stems are slid deep between her index and middle fingers. She smiles as she hands me the glass. We drink without taking our eyes off each other. I think of a first move, I have to, being the man and all, but she leans forward and kisses me on the neck. Relieved to be the prey, I keep on drinking as the pores of her wide tongue grind against my skin. I let myself fall backward on the couch while she is attempting to draw away my serum.

*The street is made of cobblestones. In the distance I notice a long set of arches. As I get closer I hear the sound of flowing water and of cart wheels scraping against the ruts in the worn-down road. I realize that the arches are a huge construction to conduct water, a sort of gigantic water pipe system in stone. I walk parallel to the water-carrying wall to find out where it leads to. Its last arch is about 1 kilometer away and is built across a wall with an entrance in it. As I get closer to this entrance, I seem to hear merchants' screams coming from the other side of the aqueduct. When I walk through what appears to be one of many numbered gated entrances, I am confronted with people wearing coarse fabric tunics in pastel colors, fastened at the waist by ropes. They are wearing leather sandals tied all the way up to the calves by long leather strings. Verandas made of striped sheets shadow the merchants' stands. I wander through this market searching for a man named Caius. There must be some kind of authority that can direct me to him in this sort of Kasbah. I move toward what seems to be a military garrison. Someone with the appearance of an angry mob moves toward me. I quickly jump to the side to avoid being caught in it but the multiple bodies rapidly spill into the market square, absorbing me. The men are raising* their fists in anger and they are all looking towards what looks like a gallows. I ask the man closest to me what is happening.

"The richest man in town, Caius, has been condemned to death," says what seems to be a peasant.

"Why?" I ask.

"Who cares? I am not the governor. I am here for the entertainment. It's not often that we see the rich suffer," says the peasant, apparently amused by my overwhelmingly caring reaction.

"What will they do to him?" this time I speak in a more detached tone.

"He killed his own mother. Lapidation. What else?" says the peasant showing me the tools of justice in his hands.

The man who must be Caius is dragged through the mob by a human chain made of guards. As he passes by, he is hit and spat on. Behind the commotion a litter carried by 4 slaves comes swiftly to a stop by a set of stairs on the other side of the square. One of the slaves only has one arm. He is at least 6 feet tall with a scar across his chest. A beautiful woman with light hair covered by a dark veil quickly gets off and walks up the stairs followed by 2 guards.

She reappears when she reaches the balcony and looks down onto the spectacle. I have a sense of déjà vu about her.

Caius is a man in his 30's and is being escorted to the guards' garrison.

*Caius' tunic, soiled by dirt and blood, is much more refined than everyone else's.*

*The white is bordered by red stitching. Pulled like cattle, his wrists bleed where he is bound by a rough cord. The mob seems to know him very well and is excited by his presence. I try to keep my position, but I am at the mercy of this mindless amalgamation of bodies. As the guards start pushing us backward, holding their lances horizontally, stones are being hurled towards Caius. People on the walkway of the city wall target the attraction with whatever they can find on the ground. Some of the stones ricochet off the guards' helmets, some hit Caius and some hit those closest to me. The crowd is now gripped by a frenzy, turning each bystander into a human shield. Someone behind me wraps his arm around my neck and pulls me backward and I instinctively lift my leg up and thrust backward.*

# 19

My foot is killing me. I realize I kicked the bed stand whilst dreaming of being in what appeared to be a Roman town. Never had I dreamt of living in another historical era. I should put some ice on my foot as the throbbing is getting stronger. I hobble to the fridge, find a Coke can and place it on the sore spot. I look around for Ginger but from the bedroom I can't see her. I stand still, in alert for noises that might come from other rooms. I don't hear anything. I call her name out but she seems to be gone. I pass my hands over my face, pressing on my eyeballs as I have a terrible headache. I am in her bedroom, naked, and I can't remember a thing about last night. My hands slide down from my chest to feel myself. Nothing sticky there. As I kneel down to put my shoes on, a vertigo overtakes me. I slowly get back up and get dressed in slow motion, compiling each article of clothing from the couch to the bedroom. I then walk around the house to see if I can find any trace of Ginger, but I remember that this is likely to be an AirBnB rental. I drag myself out of the apartment and head home, obsessively scouring my mind for images of our sexual encounter. Nothing. It's the same feeling as when I would pass out from drinking in college. I would find myself home without recollecting how I got there. I try to recall the number of drinks I've had and only remember the one Ginger offered. While on the train I get my phone and open AppYours app to leave Ginger a message, hoping she will reply and give me some clues on what I can't recollect. It's hard to camouflage what I really want to know when I have no real energy to be pleasant or cute. All I can muster is: 'Hey Ginger. Thanks for last night :) Great fun. By the way was it a strike?' I click on the submit button and close the app.

Once out of the subway I call Zac to avoid being alone. He does not seem to be in the mood to talk, so I let him go. I am upset by his attitude, since usually he hears me out when something is bothering me. Through one of the windows of a retirement home I notice an old lady sipping on a tea mug. My sense of guilt pushes me to acknowledge her, but I don't as part of me knows I'd only do it because I feel sorry for her. Here is a woman who has spent her life bringing up a family and is now abandoned. It might as well be the natural course of things, but I find it cruel all the same. Most parents spend their lives creating safety for their young, and then eventually get pushed out in the cold by those they have provided for. Doesn't make sense. Zac is that sort of safety for me. Whenever something bothers me, he is there, but I am now selfishly pushing him out of my 'emotional house'.

I call him again to find out what is on his mind. Bluntly, he tells me that he might be sick because he feels pain in his pelvis and is peeing blood. It sounds quite worrying, but I need to remember that Zac is a bit of a hypochondriac. Since I have known him he has gone through various health related paranoias. Once it was the heart, another time the brain, and then HIV. Each time I have had to convince him that he was not chronically ill. And each time he has ended up going to the doctor, getting tested, and as by script it has invariably all faded away in about a month. He is a man of great depth and knowledge, and he shows it each time I ask him for help and advice. That security seems to strangely disappear when the problems are his own. The humanity in his inability to take his own advice is heartbreaking.

"Have you seen a doctor?" I ask.

"No. I'm going tomorrow." His voice is monotone.

"You know it's nothing serious, right?"

"Who knows?" he says, which I mentally translate into 'I know already. I am dying.'

"C'mon man. It's nothing. You probably broke a capillary." I have to sound credible, as if I know about his specific problem. All he needs is something to hold on to.

"I did do some high diving at the YMCA." He seems to have grabbed a hold on me.

When I get off the phone, I realise I am in front of my building. I don't want to go in. Zac used to rub his hand on my back to warm me up. I can feel the memory. The distance between my skin and my t-shirt sparks chills when they reconnect. I lift my head to pull my thoughts up but my hands dangle. When I feel low I like to think of it as melancholia. It has an artistic potential I have yet to employ. People nowadays refer to it as depression, but deflation is more like it. I am nostalgic for my simple, foreseeable life. I feel it deflate at each exhalation. I keep on taking deep breaths but my diaphragm doesn't seem to expand.

Once I get into the apartment I turn the TV on not to feel alone. I stay clear of the living room. I look for the rum bottle, pour myself a glass and sit on the reclining couch which I have moved into my bedroom. I take out my mobile and after a tour of Instagram, Facebook and Gmail I open up AppYours to see if Ginger has replied. I want to see her again, as our encounter was like eating something you like when you have a cold and can't taste a thing. When I lay on my bed, flashes of last night's dream appear. What really unsettles me is that what I dreamt felt so real, yet so emotionally foreign.

MICHELE SCARANO

Next morning, right after I wake up, I call Zac to find out how his doctor appointment went. I know it will be the usual cry wolf situation. I am also desperate to talk to him about this overwhelming anxiety I have been feeling since Danielle died. I simply need my friend to hear me out.

"So what did the doc say?" I immediately regret the patronizing tone I just used. Silence.

"Hello?" He is pissed.

"Yes. He said I need some other tests," Zac replies.

"Why?" I ask. My prediction could for the first time be actually wrong and it upsets me.

"Couple of weeks ago I told you I saw my ex. Remember? We had unprotected sex, and after a week my dick started to burn, so the doctor stuck a gauze down the hole of my penis to check for STDs. God, I don't wish that upon anyone."

"What? Is it painful?" I let out a hissing sound and I clench my teeth.

"The closest thing as far as sensation is pushing really hard on your belly button. It's like being split apart - He's going to run a test and let me know what else I need to do."

"How about we go out tonight? You know it's going to be nothing, right? Come on, I'll take you to your favorite place."

# 20

I've always wondered what makes people, myself included, like to go to fast-food restaurants. What's there that makes a person choose it over a healthy ham & cheese, salad, or better yet a nice home-cooked meal? Of course the price, but I know that when I don't have money issues I still choose it over a healthier option. I have come up with the following reasons:

1. It's soothing for the ego. The post-war individualist culture has cultivated a self-centered ego that dislikes anything which is not a reflection of itself. A restaurant with character we can find imposing: needy waiters, the décor and the long menus with foreign words. On the other hand, you have a place where, no matter in which part of the world you happen to be, you will always find the same menu, the same décor, and no harassing waiters. This is life without trauma. All you need to ask yourself is whether you like or don't like something. Change is trauma.

2. It's about celebrating yourself. Fast-food is what we ate only on birthdays as children. When we are having a hard time we treat ourselves.

3. The drugs, man. No, not because it's called junk food but because the right chemical combination of sauces and drinks within the famous 'meals' creates a glucose dependency. A Big Mac, for example, contains 18 additives which can cause some people headaches, asthma attacks, or even hyperactivity.

Zac and I choose a table near the glass wall, where the parking lot lights mix with those of the restaurant. Zac and I have been eating McDonalds together since we were 12. This is where we used to treat ourselves when one of our parents would give us money. Zac silently unwraps his Big Mac while the lights reflect on his forehead. He is not well, and not because of his conflicting behavior, which has been deceiving in the past, but because he simply looks sick. His skin is yellowish, he has deep circles under his eyes, and he appears to be rather thin. I try to stay away from the subject and tell him about the app and the encounter I had last night. I try to sound as exciting as possible to entertain him. I haven't seen him like this since the time his grandmother died. Deep down I would like to ask him what I should do about all those memories and fears connected to Danielle that just won't leave me alone, but how can I? I tell him about Ginger instead and make up what I can't remember.

As I get into the details, my gaze falls on a girl standing on the sidewalk outside. She is handing out coupons. So far she has only handed out a few, and I wonder if she gets a commission for every customer that goes into the shop next door. I wonder if the owner watches her to check his return on Investment. Judging by her lack of enthusiasm it does not look like she will last in the job long.

When I focus on our conversation again, I notice that Zac is staring at me, at my mouth, trying hard to focus on what I am saying. I remember when he and I first moved to the city, both struggling to get used to its rules. We quickly realized that this agglomeration of buildings had no feelings or time for us. Making it wasn't easy for two country boys and that is probably the reason why we morphed into an emotionally dependent couple. We love each other like any other couple.

"Has anyone come around asking for that woman's death?" Zac asks as he adds a fry to a burger bite.

When I hear that question I hear the sound of an old cassette being rewound.

"Shit man. I only heard that the building manager was going to set up a tenants meeting for questioning to determine if anyone noticed anything suspicious. That sort of thing. Really hope no one saw us together," I reply. " I am sure it will just fade away," says Zac.

"I am doing all I can to forget. That shit fucking traumatized me. The hardest part is having to deal with the sense of guilt" I say.

What I'm dying to ask is whether Danielle death's is my responsibility. But not vocalizing that question will avoid letting the guilt loose. It will be locked somewhere in my head and of course it will escape from time to time, but I will be the only one holding the keys.

Zac changes subject and asks me if I have any pics of the girl I met. I desperately want him to check on how I am feeling, but I let it go when I recognize the disease on his face.

I extract my phone from my pocket and show Zac the photo I took of Ginger while she was turned towards the bowling pins.

"Not bad. You know, I have never had a redhead," he says.

"God Zac I need you. I need your advice. I feel so alone."

"Can't you see how sick he is? For once, you need to be there for him."

"Of course. I'll always be there for him. But did this have to happen now?"

"God. Stop being so selfish. Stop thinking about yourself all the fucking time."

# 21

My mother once said 'a man is nobody without a job.' Although I do have a job I still feel like a nobody. I remember a time when I used to be ambitious, but the system slowly got it out of me. My workplace is like one of those Discovery Channel shows on animal behavior. The few alpha males spend most of their time keeping the beta males on the bottom floors of the building or furthest away from the windows where you can see what's happening outside in the real world. Unlike in the animal world however, the physically weakest here has all the power. Call it a karma joke or an evolutionary mistake, but it looks like weakness is in need of a payback. The professional alpha male spreads his testosterone through his PowerPoint presentations. Like in politics, it is not about what you do and how well you do it but how well you sell it. It's about the perception you create of yourself like 2D cardboard. The characteristic that makes human evolution different from that of other species is communication, which, unlike from the rest of the animal kingdom, has replaced strength. The best communicator is the alpha male. Work is his/ dogma. His personal life will never contaminate the persona he has built for work, and anyone whose dedication to the corporation is not as strong as his must be done away with. In the years I have been working here, my dedication has slowly retreated from the window to the middle floor, and now to a side cubicle.

I remember the mail I received when they implemented a floor reorganization. At first it just felt like some illogical exercise to keep us 'engaged' and allow for communication to improve. Yet when I look around it feels like I was purposely cut off from everyone. I am spinning on my revolving chair, trying to let the sense of loss spin out of myself. I look down at my feet, I lift them up and when I raise them once again, I notice Todd standing right in front of me.

"Ready?" he asks.

"Yep. Meet you by the restroom." I say. I always take a piss before heading out. We walk down to the local Deli.

"Did you read the last mail?" Todd enquires.

"No. What is it about? Another budget cut?"

"Don Launder got the position after all."

"It's not about what you do, it's about the way you are perceived. He is a great presenter."

"But he went over his budget," says Todd.

"If I had done that at the time I managed a budget I would have been impaled."

"You should really get the message."

"Yes you are right. They want me to leave, but I honestly don't know what else I could do with my life."

"You could die this very moment and do you think your company or any of your colleagues would care? Listen Vince, I will not let us go on living like this. I am warning you."

"Vince, Vince?" Says Todd pointing to a newspaper on the table.

"Sorry, was thinking about something."

"Check this article out. Have you ever heard of Michael Strong? He was the CEO here at our company about 5 years ago. He left just before you came." "Maybe. Why?"

"Says here they found him dead in his garage. They suspect he killed himself. Looks like he was embezzling money."

"Well, I guess at least he had the balls to kill himself" "That's a bit nihilist."

"Well, if you want to be the man in charge, you're also supposed to be in charge of your own life.

I have much respect for someone who doesn't let his environment dictate him and eventually humiliate him."

# 22

I leave work at 6pm, right on the dot. Coming out of the subway, I decide to take a side street to get back home. There is a deli at the corner, and my apartment building is right on top of the hill. As I begin the climb, a woman turns around and takes a good look at me. One of those looks that say 'I know you are behind me.' Mrs. Trigger-happy looks like she's about to swing a pepper spray can from her key chain. I decide to stop and look at my iPhone to put some distance between us, and when I start walking again she turns around once more. Her hair is fair, straight and thin, her skin complexion transparent, her nose small. She is wearing bright red lipstick. A successful byproduct of WASP inbreeding.

I feel very much affected by what I call FWAMH (pronounced fuam), Female Walking Alone Mass Hysteria. This type of female, without much prejudice, puts innocent people like me down as full-time rapists. Only fault is having a dick between the legs. To spare myself the aggravation, I cross to the other side of the street, and think of a woman who seems to be different, Melissa. Once safe on the sidewalk, I reach for my phone again and look up Melissa's address on Google maps. Her details were listed on my call list at work. I familiarise with the location, change direction and start strolling downhill toward her apartment. According to Google it is only 15 minutes away. It's hard to admit to myself that I am willing to do anything to avoid being home alone. I will hang out with people I don't like, I will laugh at a strangers' conversations I overhear, , I will run extra errands to speak to people who think I have more important things to do, I will even call that friend who just wants to pound my ass; but I skip all of this and take it to the next level. Stalking. If you think about it, stalking is a way of punishment. I know Melissa is not interested in me, but this way I will still be able to somehow be with her. Once I get to her building I search for her name on the intercom. As I go through the range of last names I wonder what her neighbors are like. Is she friendly to them? Do they keep a spare key for her?

I wait for a resident to come by whilst I stand near the intercom to give the impression I am being expected upstairs An emo looking teenager appears at the door. Black Beats headphones on. Long bangs parted to the right cover his eye. He pulls the keys attached to his belt through a thin metal wire and opens the door. He sees me follow behind but does not hold the door for me. I manage to put my foot in front of it before it closes. I stop in the lobby and wait for the kid to get into the elevator. Once alone, I try to find Melissa's mailbox. I have to go through the names twice before I spot her last name. I peek in. Nothing inside. I decide to retreat outside and wait for her to come in. I lean on a car, in the shadow, with a good view of the building's entrance. In the dark, I adjust my sensorial perception to sound and touch and try to settle into my loneliness.

I struggle but keep away from my phone as the screen could attract attention. I need entertainment. I make up all sorts of stories about what might be going on behind each apartment's' window until I reach the top of the building. Then, as I float into a flat up there, my imagination is about to design the living room when suddenly a couch pops up and with it, Danielle. Goosebumps run from my triceps to my forearms. I slide my hands on my arms to soothe the reaction. As I cast a hopeful glance toward the building entrance I tell myself I should head back home for a drink. I am just about to make a move when the building's stairs light comes on. I decide to wait . Some of us don't need verbal communication or physical touch. Proximity, only proximity. You can take without having to give. While I search for clues that might help me identify Melissa's apartment window, I notice a silhouette, very much alike hers, emerge by the building entrance. The woman comes out quickly and with rapid steps takes a sharp right turn, back down the hill. I wait long enough to follow her at a distance of about 100 yards. The woman enters the pharmacy at the foot of the hill. I stand by a newsstand. I'm dying to know if the person I am following is actually Melissa. I pull the phone out of my pocket not to look suspicious and turn my head in different directions to give the impression I am trying to find my way. Directly across me, next to the pharmacy, in a building entrance, a security guard is looking at me. I persuade myself I am not doing anything wrong. I shouldn't worry.

I check the time on my mobile screen. 2-3 minutes have gone by. At this point I realize I might be stalking a stranger.

"No. He doesn't know I am following her."

"How could he? You are just a guy standing on the other side of the street with his phone in his hand."

"Why is he looking at me then?"

"I am a good-looking guy. Someone did say I look like Patrick Bateman."

I decide to cross the street and move closer to the pharmacy window to see if I can locate her inside. I am thinking hard of what to say should I bump into Melissa.

I decide to stand with my back to the store window. I turn my iPhone's camera on. I select the camera feature towards me so I can view myself and what is behind me, inside the store. I am looking at what appears to be

Melissa's silhouette standing in line by the register. I take a picture, enlarge it and close up on her face. Yes, it is her, Melissa. I want to go in and make it appear I have casually run into her but as I turn towards the window she seems to be gone. I approach the entrance and see her walking down the avenue. I let her gain some distance, before crossing the street to follow her on the opposite side. After about 300 yards I spot a subway entrance and figure she is heading toward it. Once I see her go down the steps into Folsom station, I speed up not to lose her. All of a sudden, just as I am about to cross the road, she appears again at street level. I freeze and push my body sideways to lean on a parked car.

*"What do I do now? She could be coming back!" "Keep on walking. Let it go."*

*"Oh c'mon I've come so far. Who knows where she is headed.*

*God I'd love to fuck her. She is so hot dressed up like that."*

Once again I take out my phone and with the reverse camera try to figure out what she is up to. She is standing, mobile phone in hand, probably sending a text before losing connection. Then, she turns towards the steps again and I hurry behind her, to the entrance and down to the platform. I see her sitting with a book in her hands on a bench at the far end of the platform. I remain by the turnstiles. Only when the train approaches, I dare to move.

Once aboard, I walk through 5 cars to reach the one before Melissa's. I get to the connecting door where I can see her through the glass window. On my right, two seated women glance at me and giggle. I look down at my pants to check if my zipper has come undone and then peer at my reflection in the window to search for food stains on my face. One of the women is Asian and the other is blonde, of course. Opposites attract.

As the train rolls on, I find the noise coming through the connecting door to soothe me. It is as if the excruciating sound is paramount and I can go unobserved. After 3 stops see Melissa gets up and approaches the sliding doors. She has a black raincoat on and her hair is loose, resting on her shoulders. She is wearing a bright red lipstick. To watch her, unbeknownst to her, sparks a warm sensation in my belly down to my groin. I feel my penis waking up. I am confused about what might be causing the reaction. When she gets off I move toward the exit and hop out shielding myself behind an oversized man. He moves slowly, carrying what might be at least 40 extra pounds of lard and I panic at the thought of losing Melissa. I stay behind him for about 10 steps until we reach the escalator. By now, she must be about 40 stairs ahead of me. When she gets rolled into the top floor I overtake my cover and run up 2 stairs at a time. Back out on the street I see her crossing the road to enter the local Starbucks.

*'What do I do now?'"*

*"I told you! Let it go."*

*"I love the way my heart is racing."*

*"What should I say if she sees me?"*

*"God, always playing parent! We can just say: 'I was passing by. God, what a coincidence.'"*

I decide to go window-shopping in the clothing store right across the street, where I can keep watch from the shop's window.

"Hello sir, welcome to Tree House," retail lingo translation for 'we know you are in the store and we are watching you.' I act as if I was interested in the t-shirts piled up on a table set by the entrance on the right-hand side. I peer through them and I spot a couple I like. I then look around to find the best way to gain a view on Starbuck's entrance. There is a big window with some mannequins in display that faces the street Leather duffel bags hang above the mannequins, held by a white sailing rope with small blue dots weaved into it. Perfect to hang myself. The rope is knotted through a climbing carabiner hooked to the ceiling. Just as I get closer to the window, the shop assistant materializes and I ask if I can view one of the bags.

"Could you follow me, please? We have them in our accessories section." She mechanically turns around and starts walking toward the back of the store.

"I am actually interested in this particular one. You know how leather is. The tone changes slightly between each piece." She stalls, spins around and smiles as if she wanted to beat me over the head with her iPad. She tells me to wait a moment as she finds the small ladder. Whilst she is away I can finally take the time to look outside and focus on locating Melissa. The shop assistant comes back carrying a ladder which she holds by the rails with both hands to make sure her nails don't get in the way. She opens it up, sighs and steps up. With some courage she leans forward and unties the knot at the handles. She then lowers the bag in my hands, blowing her hair off her face. Still facing the outside window, I place it on the ground and open it to see how it could fit with my laptop, clothes, wallet and phone.

"Actually, the color is just different from what it seemed. I was looking for something more neutral." I take about another minute to check out what else is placed by the window, then I decide to move to a nearby location as I figure Melissa is not going for take away. Once outside I turn left and find a falafel shop. I order one with yogurt sauce along with a Perrier. I sit at a window stool and as the hummus balls fry I start second guessing myself. I fear Melissa might already have gone. But just as I am about to sink my teeth into the rollup, there she appears followed by a black couple.

They walk straight to the end of the curb. My heart sinks when I see them approach the curb to hail a cab. The black woman's arm is tightly intertwined with that of her Cole-Haan wearing husband.

# 23

I wait for them to get in the cab. Then, I quickly run out to hail one myself. I jump in, praying they were stopped at one of the lights down the avenue. They finally come into view and I recognize Melissa's blond hair through the back window. I tell the driver to follow my friends.

"Yes, sir. You might want to buckle up, sir," says the albino, shifting in his seat and adjusting his glasses with his index finger. He looks at me through the rear mirror from behind his thick lenses. At each turn I ricochet from one side to the other. At each stop I bounce forward. We ride through approximately 7 blocks in silence. I try to turn the info screen encapsulated in the back of the seat off, pushing buttons that don't seem to work. I attempt to sit up from the spring-shot seat to peak on what is coming ahead, but at the first traffic light I fall backward. Once again I find myself staring at the screen images. I am about to ask the driver to help me turn off the screen, when I see Melissa's cab slow down and come to a halt by a luxury hotel. I instruct the driver to stop about 200 yards ahead of them.

I dash to the hotel entrance and once inside I slip into a newsstand situated in the hall center. I flip through books and magazines to refine my browsing technique and as I peer above the stand I can see Melissa talking to a hotel staff member at the reservation desk. The black couple has shifted to the bar. After a brief discussion at the check-in counter, Melissa joins the couple and hands them something. I can't make out what it is. Not much time goes by before she retreats to the hotel's elevator; at this point it will be very hard to find out where she is going. To my regret, I decide to give up and leave the building. Then, suddenly, the couple proceeds toward the elevator and I realize that this could be my opportunity to continue.

"Which floor?" asks the man who slightly resemblances the singer Seal. Tall, Africa-born, dark, with deep black eyes and a scar on his right cheek. Unfortunately, the couple has yet to select their floor which means I can't gamble on a number. I don't respond and with a sorry look on my face I point to my ear and stand there, looking away. The man's long index presses the number 9 while I smile mercifully. I feel all powerful, omnipotent even, since I know something they don't. I keep my head down and stare at their shoes.

Zac's theory about shoes comes to my mind and I wonder what it may mean when a couple wears the same model. Shiny, new burgundy loafers. They are standing next to each other and his right leg is juxtaposed to hers. I slowly raise my head to look at the woman and notice that her eyes are closed, her hair nutty and unkempt. The man is holding her hand tight, palm in palm.

When we reach the sixth floor the man approaches the exit, turning back to look into the woman's face, as if to reassure her. He then throws a glance at me, smiles, and guides the woman outside on the floor hallway. She takes short, insecure steps and overextends her foot to exit the lift. I move toward the panel and press the open-door button to keep the doors ajar. I wait about 5 seconds, then I step out and look for my room key. As I distress over a key I don't have, I keep my gaze ahead to find out which room they are entering. As soon as they disappear from the hallway, I quickly get to their door. #648. I turn right, then I turn left and once I have confirmed no one is around I gently rest my ear on the door.

Suddenly, from somewhere down the hall, the noise of a door being opened jolts my diaphragm to my rib cage. A woman in her 50s comes out of the room to my right and stares at me. Once again, I try to reach into my pocket to look for a nonexistent key whilst my blood meanders back to my heart from far-away destinations and my brain deflates like a helium balloon. A bell-like noise precedes the elevator's doors closure. Then, all seems quiet again. Facing room 648, I keep telling myself 'I have taken this far enough'. I slowly move away, turn and walk toward the elevator. The sliding doors open and I step forward into the out-going cleaning lady's trolley. She apologizes and informs me that the clients' elevator is the adjacent one. The small shampoo and soap bottles rattle as she lifts her cart to get over the gap between the shaft and the floor. I shift my gaze from my feet to her face and move towards the clients' elevator. The elevator's doors shut, my awareness with them and I stand there, motionless. My neck is stiff. I rest my eyes on the above digital display as it lists each floor.

When I turn again toward the hall the first thing that catches my attention is the cleaning woman's cart. I begin to walk and at each step I take, I feel my weight pressing down on the pristine carpet. I slowly sway to the side as the freshly brushed carpet gives into me. The cleaning trolley stands by room 646. The door is open so I lean my torso over the entrance's threshold to locate the cleaning lady. I hear her humming in the bathroom. Like a ski jumper, my head pulls forward, my legs follow and we reach the room's balcony. I push the curtains slightly to the side and crack the window open. Then, I slide through and pull the curtain and window back. I look over the adjacent balcony to gauge how I can reach it. A clear plexiglass divider extends from the wall to the railing.

First, I pull my right leg over the rail, then I push my body upholding onto the edge of the divider. Resting my buttocks on the railing, I lean to the right so that I can reach down with my right foot and pull my left leg over. I look around and see a reclining chaise longue with a matching white square table.

The curtains are drawn. I slowly approach the window glass doors and lean my right ear against the cold surface. A stinging sensation in my ear reminds me of where I am. I have just come so far. My heart starts pounding.

"I have found the right person for your wife, Mr. Jackson," says Melissa.

A short silence, then I hear:

"Did you get that Diane?" Silence again. "How is this actually going to work?" asks the husband.

"I need a couple of more meetings, then he will be ready. Since your wife is unable to be active in therapy given her schizophrenic state, we need someone to do it for her. This person will act as a 'conduit' to resolve the trauma that has caused her current state."

Suddenly, the terrace window on my right slides open. Like a wounded prey I stand motionless with my ear glued to the window. I pull my head back slightly to check if someone has come out on the balcony and I see the rising smoke of a cigarette butt.

"Will she continue with the regular therapy then?" Asks the husband.

"This is part of the revolutionary approach we are bringing. Your wife can carry on with the treatment prescribed by her psychiatrist, while we work in parallel. What is she on at the moment?"

"She is on a daily tablet of 900 mg of chlorpromazine, 30mg of Haloperidol, (need to add more)." The husband delivers the list which he seems to have learned by heart.

"What are her main hindering symptoms? I am sorry to be asking these questions, but they are very important to develop a proper patient profile," Melissa says.

"Well, since the beginning of treatment Diane has been reacting well to medication but she seems to through a cycle. Our psychiatrist has been trying to understand why at certain times the drugs seem to stop working. She falls into a catalepsy state and we are unable to connect with her."

" Does Diane become violent at any time?"

The man sighs. "We had to restrain her a few times when she seemed to be hallucinating. She would act as if hiding from something hitting her. Once I found her beneath the car in our garage. I tried to calm her down but when I spoke to her she replied in Latin. As far as I know she has never studied it."

I detach my ear from the cold glass window and turn toward the city view. 'Family Time Matters'. Again, that billboard. The sight of my breath condensing within regular intervals gives me comfort. I can hear the chorus from the Baptist church right below. "Jesus loved you, this much."

*"See, you fucking psycho? She's not here just to get fucked in some kinky threesome, you degenerate. She is here to help someone! Look at you sad, sad bastard. Look at where you are, on a hotel balcony like some fucking lunatic. Are you a lunatic Vince? Are you a fucking lunatic? Answer me, you fuck!"*

*"I am not. I am just here because I needed to know."*

*"You just wanted to prove that all the women you get close to are whores. So what you gonna do now? Now can you fall in love?"*

*"Maybe."*

*"Oh, shut the fuck up. All you can do is fall off this balcony."*

*"You are right, I am a sad, sad being. But I rather be here than at home alone. Alone with that fucking couch. Motherfucker!"*

Shaken by contrasting feelings, I retrace my steps back to the other balcony. I am satisfied like a teenager who has been able to get away with murder and I am worried like a parent for having watched myself going way too far with it all. I press my hands on the sliding window and slowly push towards the left to get back into the room. The cleaning lady is nowhere to be seen. I step in and as I am walking by the bathroom there she is, in front of me again.

"Soo scared. I did not hear you come in. My God!" the woman says in a Spanish accent.

"I am sorry. I had forgotten my scarf." I pull it out of my jacket's pocket and quickly get out of the room. Back to the elevator, into the lobby and out into what I can't control.

# 24

The second girl I match with on AppYours is Flora. She is 28, Chinese, 5,5 tall, really short hair. We agree to meet at a bookstore/cafe she picked. I don't see this as being your ideal blind-sex date location, but on her profile it says she loves books. Whilst waiting for her I walk around the place and start browsing through the books. I used to read a lot but I don't have the focus anymore. I notice a book with an orange cover. An image of the last book I read, 'The Circle', pops into my mind I don't seem to be able to recollect the writer's name or the story of the book. I walk to the cash register and ask the woman sitting there to point me to the bookshelf where I can find the book. She tells me to look into the Modern Fiction section. I spot it right away on the third shelf up. I pull it out and read the author's name, Dave Eggers. I open up Safari on my phone, look him up and read the book review. Modern day Orwell's 1984, it chronicles tech worker Mae, a farm town California girl who joins a tech company, Google like, which for democracy's sake, asks politicians and regular joes to livestream their lives through their website to be accountable for anything they do." As I peep into the pages, I hear the ringing of bells hanging by the entrance door. When I look up I see an Asian woman that resembles Flora's AppYours profile image. I put the book back on the shelf, turn away from the door and head to the toilet right behind the bookshelves. Once inside I stare at my reflection in the mirror. I open the faucet and wet my hands to fix my hair. When I sleep on my right side my hair folds in the wrong direction and sticks ups. I come out and find Flora by the magazine stand, flipping through a copy of The Economist.

"Flora? Hi, I am Vince." I say as I stare directly at her lips, framed by the perfect roundness of her face.

"Hey, sorry I am late." She says as she leans forward to hug me. I've read that sex with people who have symmetrical faces is more likely to produce an orgasm.

On her profile Flora describes herself as a contradiction; quiet and intense. The bio title reads 'A man doesn't know until a woman tells him.' Zac who's gone through an Asian phase says that western men confuse an Asian woman's desire of affection with sexual needs. In Asian families, display of affection is rare. When I say Asian, I mean the Confucian-influenced countries such as China, Korea, and Japan. As puberty sets in, physical loneliness sets in. Hugging, kissing, or physical contact of any kind is frowned upon. Once out of the reach of the family, an Asian woman trades sexual attention for affection.

Over the last four years Flora has been a salesperson at the airport's Hermes store. I must have seen her before, since I have been in that store a few times, given my obsession with scarves. Her bony chest is adorned by a thick silver chain without a pendant. We sit at a table by the window and when she reaches for her cappuccino, her jade bangle hits the table, sending shivers through my body. I tell Flora that when I was a child, in the summer, I would secretly sneak into my mother's room to look into her jewelry box. Hidden below the gold and silver, was a firm but delicate jade bracelet. I don't remember how I came to discover it, but I was mesmerized by how cool it felt when I would bring it to my cheeks. As if it was alive. Every other object in the house would succumb to the heat, but not the jade bracelet. I used to think that when the earth bled deep down below, it would turn into jade.

"When I was 8, my mother gave me this bracelet. It is a tradition in all Chinese families. She told me that I should wear it for life as it would first of all ward off evil and injury and then be my compass in life. Jade embodies the virtues of Confucius: courage, compassion, modesty and wisdom. It also gauges health by fading if our mood or health is suffering. And similarly to what you thought about Jade being alive, we believe that energy flows between our body and the bracelet. " Flora looks down at her bracelet, then takes a sip from the white ceramic cup. Her eyes are brown but there is a light in them I can't describe.

"What happens when it breaks? Does it mean you are sick or something bad will happen?" I ask her.

"It means that the woman could have suffered something awful, a sickness or an accident, but the jade took the damage," says Flora.

I lean backward on my chair and I move my gaze from her small feet, to her crossed legs with small bulging calves. I imagine her sitting naked with a compact pelvis resting flat with no extra fat, the thickness of her vulva undisputed between her skinny, male-like, butt cheeks.

The conversation is direct and honest, unsolicited. Flora starts telling me how she developed her appetite for sex. At 13, while rummaging through her parents' closet to try her mother's clothes on, she stumbled upon her father's video porn collection. Every day as she came back from school she would quietly sneak into the room and pick one of the tapes. Then, she would quickly grab the black VCR deck and hide it under her oversized Gap sweater.

"I would do it not as much to appease my sexual desires, but because I wanted to make sure sex was something I enjoyed since all my friends would talk about it all the time. I was too afraid to get close to a boy and watching was as much as I could bear."

The women I have had the best sex with, have coincidentally all been exposed to porn. I don't advocate it, knowing the severe effect it has had on my sexual perception. Both mental and physical. As junkies we look for one another as our needs are no longer satisfied by a partner who is into the conventional version. In the beginning, we are driven by novelties such as new positions, lingerie, dirty talking, and bukkake. Then when you have done it all, you come off the stage and you become a spectator, going back to where you began, watching. Most decide to eventually leave the theater. Few are too defined by it and must stay to repeat each line by heart.

Flora asks if I want to move on to the bar at the St. Peter's hotel and I acquiesce. We walk about two blocks and she intertwines her arm with mine. We sit at the bar and we both order a Moscow Mule. I take numerous time-taking sips as I am torn between letting the alcohol or myself fill the silence.

"Tell me 3 of your favorite animals and the reasons why you like them." Flora brings her small hand over her mouth. Her nails are long and coated deep blue. She looks at me, then up while she wrings out her animals.

"The giraffe. The dog and …..." I tell her to take her time as the third one is always the hardest.

"The tuna," says Flora as she lays both hands around her glass.

"Ok. What are the characteristics of these animals that made you choose them?" I ask.

"I like the giraffe because it is elegant. It stands above everyone with elegance. The dog because it is loyal and friendly. And the tuna, I am not sure. I just like it."

I act as if I were deep in thought. I lean backward and the lamp right behind me casts a shadow. It is big, bigger than me, dark, it judges my every move. I hold my breath to become inanimate. Then, I catapult myself forward and let the air back in, this time outmaneuvering darkness.

"The first animal represents how you want to be seen by others. The second animal reveals how people see you, and the third one is about who you really are." I explain.

"You are saying that people view me as a dog?" Flora's expression seems truly worried by this finding.

"Well, no. Symbolically they do." I smile and her lips mirror mine with about 5 seconds delay.

"It's more about the characteristics of each animal and what they stand for. The giraffe for example suggests that you want to be seen as unique. Someone that stands out, like a giraffe."

"Go on." She holds her drink up to her face and slowly caresses her cheek with it.

"The dog as your second choice, represents how people see you. They regard you as someone loyal and friendly." I think of the Asian woman stereotype and cringe.

"You know what I mean, right? It's the symbolism behind it." I smile and wait for her reaction, counting on her objectivity.

"So, the first 2 animals are about perceptions, whilst the third animal tells us who you really are. And this is when we come to the tuna. A fish, which is not a mammal and doesn't walk the earth. Let's say it belongs to another reality. But in its reality it is part of a group. Its identity is the group." After what I just said I am not sure if I charmed her or made a fool of myself.

Flora tries to pick up the lemon slide with her pinky. Beautifully slender, elegantly adorned by a gold signet ring.

"I'm from another reality? Maybe because I'm not from here?" She laughs and I exhale.

As I continue explaining the meaning of the tuna I get off the stool to get closer to her. She widens her legs while her feet rest on the foot holder. She leans over and asks me about the tattoo on my wrist. The small outline of a heart. The warmth of her breath softly penetrates my ear canal. I tell her it is there to remind me to love myself. She teases me and I suddenly feel like I need to justify myself. It is not meant in a selfish way, I mumble.

I have lost count on the drinks. To counter the compounding alcohol effect I invite Flora for a smoke outside. She holds her cigarette with her index and middle fingers extended. As I let the smoke reach deep into my chest, I notice that her black framed glass lenses are fogging up. I lean closer and with my thumbs I polish the steam away from the right frame. Then, whilst I pass my thumb over the left frame I am close enough to kiss her lips. I want to feel the softness of her lips. No tongue. I am not sure how long our kiss lasts. When we start feeling cold, we go back inside to grab our coats and head to my place.

By the elevator, as Flora presses the button up, I stand behind her and start kissing her neck. Her first reaction is to tilt her neck backward. Then she counteracts and lets me take her scent in. I follow her in the elevator. She moves to the wall and leans against it. The doors close behind me. Flora is staring at me. Her eyes are fixated on me but her awareness is inward. Her facial expression gradually shifts from concentration to disbelief as if an unknown sensation is taking over her. She puts her hand in the middle of her chest. Then, slowly, her left leg moves slightly forward and over to the right knee. I stand there and watch, until the floor bell rings. At this point, I extend my hand and lead Flora into my apartment.

Once we are inside, I excuse myself to the bathroom. I wash myself, grab a condom and put it in my pocket. Then, I join her. She is sitting on the couch, legs crossed, sipping what seems to be rum.

"I just helped myself," says Flora.

"Oh, sorry for not offering before." I say and grab the glass Flora has filled up for me. The first sip coats my throat, easing me on the sofa. She sits silently, drink in hand, and reaches for the remote. I take another sip whilst Flora is channel surfing. When she reaches level 300, adult channels begin to appear. She stops at 303. She looks straight ahead at the television screen where 2 women are masturbating each other. She slowly slides lower on the couch. With her drink close to her lips, she unbuttons her jeans using her free hand. I look at her hoping for a sign of inclusion but I perceive she on a mission. I take another sip, as I watch her sigh longer and louder. Whilst I patiently wait I feel my muscles melt at each penetration.

*After risking being hit by one of the rocks intended for Caius, the man who's pulled me away from the confusion tells me that Lavelia, a patrician, has asked for me to see her. The man, named Amilcare, walks fast ahead of me and doesn't engage in conversation. He is about 40, bald and is wearing laced leather sandals and a green tunic with a leather belt from which a coin sachet swings at each step. He leads me through small walkways towards the residential area of the city. We walk upward in the direction of a hill dominated by a villa urbana. A country seat that can easily be reached from Rome for a short stay n. As we get closer we walk by a villa rustica, the farm-house estate permanently occupied by the servants who are in charge of the estate. When we arrive at the front gate I recognize the armless guard who, along with three others, was carrying on a litter the veiled woman back in the city square. He is now standing with a lance in his right hand. He greets me with a strong Thrace accent and walks me in a big atrium. My guide remains by the entrance. There are columns at each corner, and burgundy colored curtains hanging on all sides. The slight breeze floats through the top to the flapping bottom. In front of me are small steps that seem to lead into a garden. I see a Mediterranean banana tree loaded with 4-inch bananas and a pine with a wide trunk. I walk through the trees and I notice a pool just ahead of me. I listen to the sound of water trickling in from a natural spring within a rock wall. Waterlilies cluster together right beneath it. As I stand there, I see women come my way. They don't seem bothered by my presence. They smile at me, let their tunics drop to the floor and jump into the pool. I do the same and push myself from one side of the pool toward the center. The water drags over my bulging chest. I slowly rotate my arms and legs to stay afloat.*

*Then, I swim back towards the edge of the pool. There I find a sponge which I dip in a vanilla container. I gently rub it over my arms and chest; my breasts are firm and plump, the nipples soft, not yet devastated by suckling. I recognise one of the women in the pool as the veiled lady that appeared on the balcony earlier on.*

*"Welcome to my house. I am Lavelia. Daughter of Cornelio Maluginense," says the woman. Her appearance reminds me of Melissa. "Thank you for inviting me," I say.*

*"I need you to speak to the Governor about Caius, the treasury*

*commissioner." I keep afloat as I gently move my arms in a circular fashion. "The man who has been sentenced to death? What do you care?" I say. "He will die tomorrow, and you need to save him."*

*"How can I do that?" I say as this woman resembling Melissa turns around and starts swimming toward the opposite edge of the pool.*

*"The governor has a different taste for women. You are what pleases him and you could ask him to overrule the sentence." I can't seem to be able to stay afloat and think at the same time. Lavelia swims again toward me, goes around me, and grabs my hair to run her fingers through it.*

*"The Governor is no longer pleased by a regular woman. You are the union of male and female, a rarity in this part of*

*the empire. You will need to seduce him with your receptivity
and fulfill him with your masculinity," says Melissa.*

*Time fades away and I find myself being carried on a
litter by two black slaves. We are heading towards the
governor's house. Amilcare follows on foot.*

*We reach a tall villa. Above the entrance hangs a gold
replica of a fasces, a bound bundle of wooden rods with a
projecting axe blade. To romans this is the symbol of a
magistrate's power and jurisdiction over the people, Amilcare
tells me. It seems they have been waiting for me as there are
servants standing by the side of the atrium. I am asked to sit on
a marble bench. After approximately a 20 minute wait,
appears a woman with braided hair and a silver bracelet on
both biceps. She hands a few silver coins to Amilcare, then
invites me to the second floor. Bare foot, with steps that seem to
follow an imperceptible rhythm, I follow her to a room
decorated with animal frescos. A bull, a lion, a dog, and an
eagle. Within the tablinum I recognize the statues of Diana
and Dionysus. By a candelabrum is a marble bench made of 3
lances held together at the middle. I am in the governor's study.
Here is where he meets his delegates, ambassadors and generals.
I sit on the bench and I look down at my manicured feet. Then,
I stare at my sandals' leather laces squeezing the roundness of
my tonic calves. When I look back up I see a tall, lean man in
his forties come into the room with a scroll in his hands. My
first reaction is to look down, being in the presence of such*

powerful man. I bring my head up again as I remember the importance of my objective. Marcus Augustinus sits next to me and adjusts his toga praetexta over his shoulder. An off-white robe with a broad purple border reserved to senators or magistrates. As rector provinciae, the governor is the province's chief judge. I can hear Lavelia's words about the governor having the sole right to impose capital punishment. To appeal a governor's decision would necessitate travelling to Rome and presenting one's case before Caesar himself.

"So you are Vincentia. Lavelia told me I have something you want and you have something I want. As you may imagine someone of my caliber can take what he wants when he wants. But the game is much more fun if there is an equal exchange," Marcus Augustinus says. Then stands up as he carries on speaking. "You see Vicentia, life away from Rome is so mundane and at my age it takes something exceptional to get my heart pumping fast. Pumping the way it used to when I still believed in the virtue of good vs evil. I have killed many men. With my hands, swords, lances and I have sent many to the gallows. People start to appear as mere puppets to my show. This is why every so often I need someone of your kind to tame me. It is the only way I have to avoid Nero's faith. Madness and destruction. When you are always the one in control, an hour or two of chaos bring back the fear and the desire to keep the status quo," says the governor as he tightens the scroll on his desk.

MICHELE SCARANO

*"So why are you here and what can I do for you?" Marcus Augustinos continues whilst he comes closer, sits and lays his big hand on my bare knee. Each finger is adorned by thick hair on the third and second phalange.*

*A strange rush spreads from my stomach to my chest. Being so close to his power arouses me. Part of me hardens and part of me becomes wet.*

*"I am here to ask you to spare Caius' life." I cross my legs and his hand slides off.*

*"Ah, Caius. He is certainly a character. It will be difficult. He has wronged many people."*

*"I know, but I am here to do good by him. Killing him would not make amends. He needs to live." I take hold of his hand and bring it between my legs.*

*"Save him," I whisper as he squeezes me.*

*"Why save him? You are not one of those cult followers, are you? What do they call themselves? Christians. Pity does not become a pretty woman like yourself." He gets up, walks forward to the parapet, looks onto the garden and says: "I need a good cause to stop the execution. Caius' crime is the most hideous of crimes a, and I need a good reason to save his life. These are days of unrest, we are recovering from a long war, our grain reserves are dwindling and our people are hungry. An execution is an entertainment opportunity we need to*

~ 170 ~

*appease them. For about a week. How much of a good cause are you?" He says whilst my silence is nothing but curtesy.*

# 25

"**B**yron, it's Vince." I am sitting on the couch armrest, my right hand caressing the leather obsessively. Flora is gone. I bring my right arm in front of my chest and place my hand on my left bicep.

"Hey man, what's going on?"

"Wanted to know if you are still in town," I say.

"I'm giving a lecture at the Ashram on Folsom Avenue." "Can we meet? I need to talk to you."

I place the cell phone on the small table and with my nail I am scratching, in circular motion, the couch back rest.

Byron blends in well in the rustic background of the tapas restaurant, his warm smile and chubby cheeks a reminder of what hope looks like. He first slaps the meat and guacamole on the flabby tortilla, then mechanically sucks all of his fingers before taking a bite. Something I find disturbing and appealing at the same time. I tell Byron about the weird experiences I have been having. Waking after having spent a night with a woman and not being able to recollect a thing. And the resuming dream of what seems to be a past life.

"From what you are telling me it seems like the dreams have started to appear when you began to sleep with these women from the app community."

"Yes and I am just feeling a bit overwhelmed. The dreams happen after I sleep with them. Which as far as I'm concerned , does not even mean I fucked them since I can't remember a thing. The dream I had last night was pretty weird. I was in a pool and I had breasts and a penis. I was an hermaphrodite that in exchange of sex needed to save a man's life. Not sure if I was a prostitute or some sort of martyr." My thumbs are held by my palms.

"What I find most interesting is that the dreams you have described don't just come to anyone. Trained Buddhist monks seeking reincarnated lamas or Australian aborigines seeking knowledge from their ancestors speak of such dreams. As far as I know it is rare that we dream of our past lives. In the western world these dreams are elicited through past life regression hypnosis, which allows you to regress to other lives you have lived. It's peculiar that this is happening without any stimulation and even more that you are able to go back to the same period of time more than once."

"'Weird' is a better description, and it feels like I am going places I shouldn't, like a sleepwalkers. You go to sleep a worrying that your body will be doing something you don't want it to do. Everything feels so real. And let me tell you, it's a bit unbalancing to find yourself having both sexes."

Byron stays silent, then picks up his Samsung as if going through emails, which I find rather annoying.

"I might know someone that can help you," he says, still looking at his device.

# 26

Z ac's parents act younger than their age. I've always
had a great relationship with them, possibly the
relationship I would have wanted with mine. They
greet me at the door, smile politely, ask me how I am doing
and how far I've come with the book I started to write 5
years ago. When I compare them to my parents and when
I think about the ways in which Zac and I differ, trust is
what has made the difference.

Trust for being there even if the grades weren't great,
if there were no athletic achievements or career success. Like
guides, they were there through the path without stunting
or overshadowing Zac's assertion for his own identity. After
welcoming me like one of their own they tell me Zac is up
in his old room. When I look up at the stairs of this two
floor house I am faced with my past. Each step is a chapter
of my, 'our' childhood. Each step collects chronological
details of memories stashed away long ago. Running down
with cleats on our way to football, dragging kegs up on the
balcony when Zac's parents were away, sliding down with
a snowboard while on acid. Funnily enough, 15 years ago

these stairs did not seem to exist. Our excitement to get from point A to point B was so overwhelming that what stood in between was only time, not things. Now, each step becomes heavier and heavier with all the baggage I have collected.

"Looking for porn again?" I say when I slowly push the door open to find Zac typing on his computer.

He turns around, smiling, knowing too well from the sound of my steps that it is me. His smile, his lips quickly fade in the paleness of his skin. He gets up from his desk and sits at the side of his twin bed. He is wearing a sweatshirt from an awesome 1992 Iron Maiden tour. It's alarming to see how his demeanor has changed in a few days, let alone since we were stage diving at the concert 10 years ago. It's the speed at which he moves that presents reality in its barren self. It is like powerlessly watching someone take his manhood. The slow motion in which a Praying Mantis eats its male partner after copulation.

"What's up Zac!?" I say with conviction to force life into the room. "Did my parents tell you?" The tone of his voice is as loose as the sweatpants he is wearing. I know where he is going, but I am rejecting every thought of it. The only person that lived on my frequency is about to go off the air. I frantically turn my mind dial to search for a station, but static is all around me.

"How are you feeling? Still thinking about that woman ?" asks Zac as he takes a sip of his cinnamon tea.

"Not really - a dark hole opens in my chest as I think of Danielle - I've been seeing a couple of girls. You know how that takes my mind off everything." My lips stretch to smile, but the rest of my face is frozen. I start telling him about Jade and Flora and make up the sexual details to get him excited and involved. Zac pulls himself against the bed's head stand and then slowly slips down with his head on his pillow.

I get up, walk towards the bookshelf and look through his coveted Marvel comic collection. There is one particular comic called Civil War that always fascinated me, where superheroes split in two opposing factions. Captain America fights Iron Man to keep mutants out of a government identification program. I skip to the last page to see who makes it out alive. If I could be any of these characters who would I be? The Hulk. Passive-Rage. I turn around and see that Zac has drifted off to sleep.

# 27

When I get back home a strong sense of loneliness hovers in the air, in between objects, as Lyonel over the concrete floor. It is a different type of loneliness to the one I am used to. It slithers r inside my mind, brain, body, eyes; a sound, like a muted vibration that makes my body feel as if it's wearing an armor a size too big. It's like the black substance that takes over Spiderman in one of the recent movies. Peter Parker's body is slowly covered in an alien substance that transforms him into an anti-hero. Everything that is supposed to be familiar feels foreign and distant. Loneliness is a cold draft that enters through my mouth and cuts my heart in two.

I look at what is supposed to be home. It is nothing but a box made of cold concrete. Can a heart pump in concrete? I slide into bed, hoping to recall the feeling of warmth, belonging and protection, but my thoughts selfishly keep the blanket for themselves. I look around the room. The Gauguin painting, the clothes hanging in the closet, the baseball cap on the dresser. They are my things but they don't belong to my emotions. Nothing around me cares about me. I could die and no one would come looking for me now that Zac is unwell.

I get up to shrug off the negativity and get away from my head. I walk into the dining room, get my laptop and bring it to the bedroom. I check the New York Times home page and a side banner is flickering a face of a man who is promoting a car. As I scan the page looking at the different articles I feel as I am being watched. The man in the banner is staring at me. I quickly slide the page down to avoid his eyes and once he is away I tell myself he can't possibly be looking at me. I get up, grab a glass and pour myself some rum. I let the liquid slide down my throat and asphalt the anxiety sparks going off in my stomach. I walk into my bedroom and reach out for my phone on the dresser to see if I have made any connection on the APPYOURS app. I click on the app icon and when the screen loads up I see a small red bubble over the connections icon indicating a new match. Catalina is 37 years of age, from Spain, as she proudly underlines in her profile intro. I slide through her additional profile photos and she seems like what I need. Positive energy, intensity and an accent that fills up the gap in my stomach. I message her to see when she is willing to meet.

"Hola Catalina! Good to 'meet' you. Been training today?" I ask her about training as on her profile she has mentioned she is a big CrossFit fan.

"Hey Vince. Just back from the gym. Tough workout but I love to look at myself right after it to see how it pays off. What are you up to? "

"I just finished doing some power yoga. Now off for a bike ride. Love to get lost in the city. You've been city exploring?" I say.

"It's actually my job. I am a tour guide. What do you do?"

"I work for an insurance company but I am also a writer." I don't want to lie but I did start writing a story about 5 years ago.

"I have always wanted to write a book but work is too busy to get my head around it. Would love to hear more about it when we meet."

"Great. How about tomorrow? Coffee?"

"Well, if you have time I wanted to invite you on one of our tours." "Ok. Sure. Where?"

"Come to Odeon Hotel at 17:30. Get a ticket at reception."

When I get to the hotel lobby, I find what I imagine is the tour group waiting at reception. I approach the counter to buy a ticket. The woman in charge asks for my last name and hands me a name tag. When I enquire about the price she replies "It's free," forcing the f as if to highlight that I should know better.

While waiting to be called up by our driver, I try to avoid any sort of exchange with the rest of the group. As I'm looking at my Instagram, a scent of patchouli invades my nostrils. The smell convinces me to turn around to catch sight of thick, curly hair belonging to a small, shapely woman. I'm glad to hear that a heavy Spanish accent is coming from the same mass of hair. Ticket in hand I sit on a nearby couch and placidly let myself fall into an inspection of what is in front of me. I focus directly ahead of me and an old painting with a lamp right above it catches my attention. A fake antique to recreate Victorian-like furbishing. When I sink my gaze deep into the painting, a sense of déjà vu comes over me. I look away to let the feeling abide, to try and recall where I might I have seen the image before. Nothing comes to mind so I look around the room but end up looking forward again, at the painting. I stand up, and as I get closer to it, my head turns like that of a dog hearing a sound it doesn't understand. The image is of an ancient building with a square, on its facade the letters 'ROMA ANNO IIIV'. I tilt my head back straight as I try to manage the confusion the image is causing in me. It is the same square that appeared in my dream when I saw

Caius being dragged by the roman guards. I put my hands on the arm rest and try to pull myself out of this double reality. As I am about to lock my elbows a vortex drags me back down. A vacuum pulls everything I see into my gut, like a drain, leaving a sensory void around me. Only my thumping heart reminds me that I am.

"Anyone for the Catchstars tour please follow me," says the curly woman who heads out holding up a selfie stick. People start to slowly flow outside, and I follow behind to get on the bus. Once everyone is settled in their seats, the guide appears at the front, and speaks into the microphone.

"Hello everyone, I am Catalina and I will be your tour guide for today. First of all, I would like to thank you for having joined the 'Catch a star' tour. For those of you who are new I will quickly tell you how the rest of the day will run. As I speak, my smartphone is being tracked via GPS. This data is then uploaded to our mobile app. There, our community members throughout the city report sightings of stars, which are signaled within the app map. We are proud to say that we are the first live tracking celebrity app. Of course all of this is possible thanks to our community. You are now also part of this great family. So after today remember to share any sightings.

Now back to the serious stuff. If you haven't already downloaded our app, you can see on the screen above our celebrity tracking map which will help us locate and approach our targets. If you would like to download the app now, please go to Google Play app store for Android phones or Apple's App Store for iPhone and search for CatchStars. Spelled as the name of the tour."

Catalina turns toward the small screen hanging from the bus ceiling. She points at the red dots to indicate the last celebrity sightings.

"I have to warn you. Not all sightings turn out to be successful. It's a bit like a city safari and the animals are unpredictable and good at camouflage. It takes patience but it is worth the reward. When we are lucky it's like a corrida. We lock them in, circle them and launch in for the estocada". She mimics the movement of the torero before it plants the sword between the bull's shoulders.

"Today we are an exceptionally big group, and I hope we can all move quickly to cover as many locations as possible. Please stay close to one another as we can only succeed if we move at unison. Should you be late getting on the bus from a location, for example, and we've spotted a Rhodium somewhere else, we will leave you behind - she emphasizes her last words by creasing her forehead - it is all in the terms and conditions you signed online. This is how this tour made the N1 spot on the What To Do in NYC in the last 3 years. If you'd like to review the celebrity classification please look on page 3 of your handout or on the Celebrities link on the app. Stars are categorized by precious metals according to their recognition. The recognition level is defined by a CatchStars custom algorithm which brings together daily social mentions of the sighted individual. The levels are Palladium, Platinum, Iridium and Rhodium." Our guide stops speaking, puts the mic between her legs and ties her hair in a ponytail.

"Our target is Hollywood stars, singers or politicians. Lately we have also targeted some Youtubers and famous fashion bloggers. We have occasionally tracked some athletes but they tend to be fast and potentially uncooperative. The same goes for rap stars. Great. Now as far as the logistics go, once we have a confirmed a sighting, we will break in two groups. One will come with me, and one with Rene, our fantastic driver." She puts a hand on his shoulder and continues telling us where we are headed.

There are 12 of us, and we are tightly pressed in an A-TEAM-like black van. It has tinted windows and a black matted logo on each sliding door. The logo portrays a man dressed as a detective that runs after small stars with a butterfly net, and below it a URL www.catchstars.com.

Catalina walks down the 4 rows of seats, stepping sideways, giving out what seems to be a handout. I watch her gaze linger on all the men as if she was looking for the one she has invited on APPYours. Her eyes are dark, round, framed by a strong eyeliner. As I wait for my turn to receive the handout, I look at the guy next to me and realize he is quite handsome. Will she hope, think, that he is the stranger she is meeting? Does she remember my profile pic? My hair is shorter now.

"How did you hear about this tour?" I ask him.

"A friend invited me," he replies with a smile.

"Is Catalina 'the friend'? Will she pick him? Are we all here for her?"

"Well, if you weren't such a fucking loser you wouldn't need to know. Look at you! Do you realize what we are doing? We are on a bus with a bunch of fucking nerds. Are you this desperate? Vince I told you. You are pushing it. I can't let you go on humiliating us like this."

"Did I take her seat?" I prod further.

"No, she couldn't make it." As my diaphragm contracts, my lower gut explodes with an adrenalin rush, signaling me to get out of the bus. I lift my head and take a deep breath in to remind myself that the feeling is illogical, another panic attack. I extend my arms forward to touch the seat in front of me and my legs dig deep into the ground as if grasping for control through a flight's turbulence.

"How many sightings are they guessing for today?" I ask as I have ripped the label off my Coca-Cola bottle. The van rides through the street compressed, dense, intense. Like a juggernaut it ploughs through anonymity.

The speakers crackle as we hear Catalina listing a series of streets. "Our first confirmed target is on Babel Street. We will be stopping in about 7 minutes." She has now turned around, facing us as she speaks. She is wearing a wireless mic with a Bluetooth headset.

"At the moment I have 4 readings on the star locator." She is sliding her index over her iPhone whose screen is reflected on the bigger hanging screen behind her. It lists the names of the people spotted. In order of proximity we have actor James Spader, former NBA star Dennis Rodman, artist Christo, and actor Viggo Mortensen. The van starts to slow down pulling over in a side street.

"We know James Spader is shopping at the clothing store you see across the street. As explained in the hotel lobby, we would like you to be as reactive as possible. This is one of the reasons we have an age cap on the application form. You will see that we will have to do some running and some ducking." She puts on her tight green Avirex bomber and re-adjusts her headset.

"Those sitting on the left rows, will be coming with me. Those on the right rows will join Rene. As described on the handout, I will call on different Roman army formations. Please take 2 minutes to read the handout and familiarize yourself with how you are expected to behave when we are on recon mode. I will be referring to formations whenever we are to approach a target, so keep the handout handy. Also let me remind you, again, this is also on the handout, the closer you approach the target, the greater potential of trouble with the law. CatchStars is not responsible once you are off the van. We suggest you keep a 30 feet distance to be safe. If you want to get closer, please wait until everyone has taken their picture, and then go for it at your own risk. Be aware that the van will leave at 18:15. Please make sure your watches are synched with the bus monitor."

I have been keeping an eye on Catalina and jotting down notes on the back of the handout. How many time she speaks to whom, how long her smile lasts, whether anyone touches her. This will help me figure out at the end of the day if we all are part of the 'game' or if I am the one she wants.

1. 'Guy on third row, right aisle, has spoken to her three times, no touching, no smiling.

2. Fifth row, left window, asked her 2 questions, helped her up with her bag, and she smiled at him for 3 seconds.

3. Guy next to me has spoken once (asked what time the tour will end), no touching, Catalina smiled at him once for 2 seconds before turning around.

4. Female on first row, right aisle, has hugged her once, smiled 3 times for 2, 3, and 2 seconds.

While we stake out James Spader, J.S., the code given to our target, Catalina has alighted the van to scout the location. She's comes back after 20 minutes with a 'negative.'

"It turns out to be a decoy, a look-alike," Catalina says in a cold military tone. She gets back on her phone to brief us on our new target which appears to be Viggo Mortensen, V.M., spotted at the Excelsior Hotel's bar.

Catalina starts reading off her cell phone what seems to be a short bio of the man as his picture appears on the screen behind her.

Viggo Peter Mortensen, Jr. (Danish: October 20, 1958) is a Danish American actor, poet, musician, photographer and painter. He made his film debut in Peter Weir's 1985 thriller Witness, and subsequently appeared in many notable films of the 1990s, including The Indian Runner (1991), Carlito's Way (1993), Crimson Tide (1995), Daylight (1996), The Portrait of a Lady (1996), G.I. Jane (1997), A Perfect Murder (1998), A Walk on the Moon (1999) and 28 Days (2000).

Mortensen's career rose to new heights in the early 2000s with his role as Aragorn in the epic film trilogy The Lord of the Rings. In 2005, Mortensen won critical acclaim for David Cronenberg's crime thriller A History of Violence. Two years later, another Cronenberg film Eastern Promises (2007) earned him an Academy Award nomination for Best Actor. A third teaming with Cronenberg in A Dangerous Method (2011) resulted in a Golden Globe Best Supporting Actor nomination. Other well-received films in recent years have included Appaloosa (2008) and the 2009 film adaptation of Cormac McCarthy's novel The Road.

Catalina's mic makes a loud thump as she tries to adjust it before speaking again. "Viggo is one of my favorite targets and I have spotted him before. He is a true renaissance man. Most celebrities cultivate artistic interests outside of their careers, but Viggo could easily stop making movies and become a singer, a painter, a poet. You might not know that he was the one who composed some of the Lord of Rings music and sang it! He's a professional artistic photographer and abstract painter, who gets his work displayed in proper art galleries. He has also been writing poetry for 15 years in three languages." She ends her sentence by pushing herself up on her heels with an expression of pure satisfaction.

After the fun stats we move to the serious stuff. Catalina goes on to brief us on the strategic formation to get close to this particular star. "We need a 'skirmishing' formation, which simply means entering the hotel bar divided into couples that get in at different times. This will allow us to easily position ourselves as close as possible to the target without being recognized as a group." I wonder who on earth came up with these definitions. Once inside, we are to all sit down at different tables. If the waiter approaches before the photo opp, we are advised not to order but to buy as much time as possible within the 45 minutes available for this stop. After we have all synchronized our watches, we are distributed into couples according to where we are seated. Very last thing before getting off the van is the checklist.

"Cameras? Handout? Mobile number in case of an emergency? Pen and paper for autograph? If you do not have a pen we have some here for only 5 dollars." Catalina lets each couple off the van in about 5 minutes intervals. We need to walk about 50 yards down the traffic light to then cross to the other street and carry on for approximately another 200 yards. The hotel is on the left. At first, my partner and I walk side by side, about two feet distance between us. I take a last glance at Catalina's hand out describing the Skirmishing Formation which requires us to get as close as to rub shoulders.

Once in the hotel lobby, we walk to the bar and find the other couples queuing at the entrance where a hostess is showing guests to their tables. When it is our turn, my co-pilot puts his arm around my shoulder. I don't know what to make of the sudden show of affection. We are seated 2 tables behind V.M., with the toilettes hallway behind us. Not to arise any suspicion, as listed on the handout, I take out my camera and appear busy going through the images on the LCD screen. After my partner and I have ordered 2 cappuccinos, I notice the rest of the 'Catchers' look to my right as this is where Catalina is sitting, alone. She will be the first to get up, signaling that the hunt has begun. I look around. Everyone has their cameras and phones ready. Viggo seems unaware of what is about to be unleashed on him and continues reading his paper. Catalina brings her hands to her face to pull her hair backward. She straightens her back and pushes her plexus forward. She then gets up, iPhone in hand, and as she walks by Viggo she shoots a photo and walks towards the exit as if nothing has happened. Viggo does not seem to have noticed her and carries on reading. All the couples scope each other to understand who will be next as if forgetting the proximity rule. Who's closest goes next. My partner and I are next. Don Jonson, that's who he reminds me of, sporting a Miami Vice looking suit jacket, springs up but being too close to the table, hits it with his belt buckle causing my cappuccino cup to tip. I try to clean up whilst Don, unphased, proceeds toward the target who is sitting with his back to us. When he reaches V.M.'s table he side steps to align with V.M.'s chair, crouches to get his head close to our target and pushes his reflex camera away from him to take a selfie with our celebrity.

Viggo raises his head to find a camera held in front of him by an outstretched arm. His expression molds from bemusement to a compassionate smile. He doesn't turn to acknowledge the personal space intruder and with grace goes back to reading. Another CatchStars couple, sitting on my right, behind the target's seat, gets up and slowly approaches his table. They forgo the inclusive threesome selfie. Instead, they split and close in on both of the target's shoulders. They opt for the ruthless celebrity background selfie. They circle VM's table to face him straight ahead. Viggo watches perplexed as the couple then turns. With their backs to him, they retreat holding a selfie stick, calibrating the best angle. Viggo is holding his paper with both hands, looking on. I stay in my chair, too ashamed to get up, but envious of the selfie Catchers' pragmatism. As the third couple moves forward Viggo puts his paper down and waits calmly to be shot. I get up and acting indifferently I head towards the exit. Proud to be above it all. My left index finger's nail digs deep into my thumb's cuticle.

Catalina high fives everyone as we get back into the bus. She announces that we will now move onto Christo's traces. The guy behind me, who is wearing a photographer's vest, says "Who is he? A cult leader?" and of course everyone laughs. Christo is a seventy something Bulgarian artist known for creating environmental works of art by wrapping major historical locations in fabric. His bio appears on the screen. Christo's works include the wrapping of the Reichstag in Berlin and the Pont-Neuf bridge in Paris, the 24-mile (39 km)-long artwork called Running Fence in Sonoma and Marin counties in California, and The Gates of fabric in New York City's Central Park.

We are all relieved to discover that it is another decoy and that former NBA star Dennis Rodman has been spotted at a golf store on the corner of LaFayette and Davison. The van stops about 700 yards ahead of the store. It is around 19.10. Everyone springs out like a bunch of weekend skydivers to land in the tortoise formation. We walk quickly, packed together, until we are 300 yards away from the golf store. In the tortoise formation or testudo in Latin, the men align their shields to form a packed formation covered with shields on the front and top. At about 150 yards from target lockdown, Catalina, at the head of the group, signals to stop by lifting her arm clenching her white iPhone in a tight fist. We are to change into the Orb formation, which means lining up at increasing numbers. 1, 2, 3, 4, 5.

Catalina selects me to go in for recon. She tells me that she has already been in this store for another sighting and wants to avoid being recognized.

"Ok, you go first. Once you are inside, look for signs of store security or celebrity bodyguards. I remember there being 3 exits, but you should double check. Finally, evaluate if the customers could be an issue to access our target. What's app me with a quick review." I jot down her number and move toward the entrance of the store.

By the door, a couple of guys who must be in their late twenties remind me that my view of the sport might be a bit outdated. I walk around the paraphernalia with amateurish interest. I move further into the store. The two kids I saw at the entrance are busy pulling out clubs of various shapes while they ask each other if they need this number or the other.

I take out my phone and start messaging Catalina.

"There are a couple of kids looking at clubs and some old guys looking at balls. Customers would not be an issue for our group.

So far, no sign of big men in suits, sounds of walkie-talkies, or Dennis."

Upstairs I find the mechanical side of the sport; multiple machines that are supposed to help your swing are aligned throughout the open floor. At the far end of the large room, a huge glass wall gives onto the street above the street entrance. As I get closer to the glass I notice the silhouette of a man swinging on a green mat by the right corner. Here is Dennis, alone, concentrated, aligning his 48 sized feet with his face looking down, clenching the club. I take a photo and send it over to Catalina. Then, I walk back to the stairs where I can view the entrance and see the Catchers slowly trickle in. Whilst I stand there in silence, the sets start to pile up with their iPhones and cameras. Rodman keeps swinging, unaware of what is happening behind him. As the people-jam coagulates, Catalina, seeing the target with a golf club in his hands, warns that this target is highly unpredictable and that the mission is aborted. The woman who sits on the third row of the bus, wearing a CrossFit t-shirt, does not agree with the decision and breaks away from the group with pen and paper in hand. Rodman, about to pull the club backward feels her tapping him on the shoulder. He turns his head, then lowers it down to locate her. He brings the club back to par and stares at his feet for about 5 seconds. The woman is standing, shifting her weight from the left to the right hip. Rodman lifts his head and as the woman is about to invade his space with pen and paper, lets the club drop and walks away without saying a word. When he walks by me, down the stairs and to the cashier, I hear him say:

"Please have the stuff ready for pick up. Someone will come by for it." Once our celebrity is gone Catalina tells everyone to gather back to the van for a 20 minutes takeoff.

"Hmm, hmm. Can you hear me? It is unfortunate that we had to abort this mission. As I had mentioned previously some celebrities represent a high-risk factor especially if they hold a golf club in their hand. Our tour has come to an end and I would like to thank you all for joining us and our community. We hope to see you back soon, and don't forget to report any sightings to our app. 'Once a Catcher, always a Catcher.' Oh, one final thing, if you'd like to find out about our other tours, feel free to stop by our office at the hotel."

Once we are back at the hotel, at around 20.45, I decide to let everyone off the bus first, giving them time to disperse. In the hotel hall a woman in a green uniform seems busy pulling dead leaves off of a spider plant. When her water spray falls off her belt, I bend forward to pick it up. As I am about to get back up, blood swerves from my head down to my chest. My head is drained, I am a dwindling rock stack waiting to collapse. Luckily, the lady grabs me by the elbow and sits me on a nearby couch.

"I'm fine, thanks. Lost my balance there for a second." I bring my hands to my face as if to wash away what just happened. When I release the pressure off my eyes, a shiny shape appears, slowly morphing into Zac's face. I try to focus on my surroundings and images of Danielle, Caius, Flora sprout on each side of my brain. Like a building on fire, I want to throw the thoughts out of my head as flames ravage below, through my chest. The physical loss of balance turns into a sensation of detachment. I am vanishing away into a mind's black hole. I open up my palms onto the couch to ground my panic.

"What's happening to me? God I need help."

" You don't need help! You just need to man up and start looking for a real woman. Enough of this bullshit. You dragging through these ridiculous dates. Fuck this! I thought you could do better than this."

"This is not helping. Fuck. I need to be well. I need to calm down. Focus on my breath."

"Focus on how fucked up you are. You are desperately trying to get laid but I haven't felt one single orgasm. Have you?"

If you get gangrene, they save you by cutting your arm off. If you have high blood pressure, you get pills to reduce it.

Medicine has slowly unlocked all the complications of the human body. The mind remains terra incognita, and I feel ever more like a cast away.

# 28

I land on the reception desk, breathing in deeply and pushing out unwanted thoughts. I ask for the tour guide, and I am asked for my name.

"Vince," I tell the receptionist, a woman in her fifties. Her hair is twirled in a bun and she is wearing strong red lipstick. A bit overweight but beautifully manicured nails.

"Vince what? My dear." Her expression tells me she's got better things to do than dealing with me.

"Zemolo," I say with a questioning tone that I regret.

I am given a key card and I am told that Ms. Extebarria is expecting me in room 424.

I slide the key card about 4 times before the light on the door handles turns green. I press it down and I hear the air in the room being sucked into the corridor.

"Hello?" Like a sonar I let my voice search for Catalina in the unlit room. No reply. I move forward, scanning empty closet and the closed bathroom door. I see her clothes dropped randomly on the sofa. Lace. I don't like lace. Traditional, conventional, reactionary. It belongs to a time when sex was rare and a man was so horny that even when the woman didn't happen to be in great shape, he became aroused by the teasing of the holes in the fabric.

The bathroom doors open slowly, and the trajectory of a dim light shines in my direction.

"You made it chico. Bath is ready. I always take one after a tour, my feet get so sore." I admit I wasn't thinking of getting so cozy right away. A bath is more intimate than having straight-up sex. It's sensual. It requires patience, attention, control. But we are not such strangers after all. I know she has been watching me throughout the whole outing I feel shy as I take my clothes off. I stare at her to force her gaze away. The water is up to her neck, her hair is tied together and her eyes stay closed. There is foam covering all of her body, but her round, rigid, breasts stand above water. I slowly dip in, holding my upper body with my hands on the side rims, sliding around her legs to find space. I feel her goose bumps as I brush against the outside of her calves. The heat of the water feels claustrophobic at first, but as her foot slides over my inner thigh desire pushes all other sensations away. I look at her face for guidance, but she remains expressionless. The neck of her foot slides and brushes up and down my legs, moving from one side to the other. Blood flows to my penis like air to a blow-up buoy that's been pushed under water by a wave. It sways with the current generated by her movements, causing it to stroke my pelvis. At each self-stroke, vulnerability and surprise become a new erotic sensation.

We are two intertwined octopuses, testing, dancing. I drag my arms back, place my hands next to my chest and push my torso upward. I feel the cold air swerving around me as I lean forward to slide my body over hers. I feel the foreignness of her breasts and grab onto her familiar ass cheek. I kiss her lips, hiding behind her closed eyelids while her tongue slowly advances to twist with mine. Our bodies shift sideways, turning like mating snakes. When the water gets cooler Catalina rises, letting the water drip off her body onto me. In slow motion, she wraps a towel on her head and another one around her body; only to unwrap herself once on the bed. Like a pastry she lies on her foil cup, sipping on a drink, waiting for me to taste her. I clumsily get on the bed at its foot, crawling to take a position next to her. The front window reflects how unsexy I look as I pull my naked body onto the nylon blanket. I lay restless, conscious of my appearance and of the cold texture below. She hands me her drink over and I accept it for warmth and disappearance.

*I am laying in bed, the room is wide and I can feel a soft breeze coming in. The ceiling is high and the fresco on it portrays Hermaphroditos, a minor Greco-Roman deity of unions, androgyny, marriage, sexuality and fertility.*

*I lower my eyes and see next to me, asleep, the governor Marcus Augustinus.*

*I feel contrasting emotion toward this man. Part of me wants to slowly dip under the cover and wake him laying my tongue on his masculinity. Another part of me wants to grab his neck, turn him sideways and invade him. When I start to softly caress his chest and nipples, he wakes. Looking up again at the fresco on the ceiling I start whispering to him the story behind Hermaphroditos' legend. "The story goes that Hermaphroditus was brought up by naiads in the caves of Mount Ida, a. When he was fifteen, he encountered the nymph Salmacis in her pool. She tried to seduce him but was rejected. The nymph came out of hiding, jumped in the pool and wrapped herself around the boy calling on the gods that they should never part. Her wish was granted and their bodies blended into one."*

*"Vincentia. I have found a way to spare Caius' life." The governor has opened his eyes and seeks my body with his hand. He reaches behind my back and pulls me onto him. From above him I can see the scars on his chest and neck. As I adjust my pelvis over his, he brings his right hand over my mouth and forces his index and middle finger in my mouth. I let him, until his family ring hits against my teeth. As I begin my tidal movement he speaks.*

*"I will organize a gladiator's fight and invite Micero to speak. You know how people love him. He is the greatest orator*

*of our time and will be able to convince the populace to change their minds about Caius. He will speak before the beginning of the fight and once the people will have accepted our trade, I will not be judged to be lenient on Caius."*

When I wake up it's 1:23 a.m. I touch the mattress beside me, and it still feels warm. The dream I just had flashes before my eyes. A sense of shame comes over me. I get up and catch a glance of myself in the mirror. My first reaction is one of confusion. I know it's me, but an unsettling feeling is stirred by the recollecting images of my dream. I walk back in front of the mirror to comfort myself, to convince myself I am not who I was in the dream.

"Catalina? Catalina, where are you? Catalina, where the fuck are you?

This can't be happening again. Wait. What was that dream about?

That roman shit again. Ohh, god - was it me having sex with that guy?

What in the name of Jesus is happening to me?!"

*"I knew this was a bad idea. I seriously need to take control here." "I am really trying hard here. I can't be alone. Can't you understand? It's makes me so sad. I am trying real hard and what do you do? You just fucken take me down and judge everything I do."*

*"Vince, what you need now is me hurting you. Because that is real.*

*You need to be reprimanded for this shitshow you call your life."*

*"Shut up. Shut up! Why is this happening to me? What have I done to deserve this?"*

*"You are just a weak motherfucker. You should be in a normal relationship. But we can't have that, can we?"*

*"Tell me of a woman who would want to date a man like me. Look at me. I am in a fucking hotel room. Alone. And I don't even know if I got laid."*

*"You know you didn't. Vince, I told you, what you need now is me hurting you. You deserve it. I am tired of you humiliating me like this." "No. Please don't."*

My lower chest springs up and my heart start racing to bring the oxygen I am unable to keep inside. I grab the drinking glass on the dresser. My anger overrides my fear and I drive the bottom part into my right temple. Pain comes at the same time as the surprise of a new emotion.

I try to smooth the pain away by rubbing my cranium with my hand, yet the satisfaction for achieving punishment remains.

"You see Vince, you can get what you want when you let me be in charge."

I then look at myself in the mirror, comb my hair with my hands. I can see myself smile, but I am good at hiding it. I have found a way to take control.

I tuck my shirt in, wash my hands and go on to call out for Catalina. Once again I am alone with the recurring dream. I need grounding and I grope for Melissa's phone number.

# 29

"Pagoda at Hamilton Park, 1:30 p.m.?" I agree to meet Melissa because I have a desperate need to share what just happened. I am outside the building but I need to get back to the apartment twice. First time to get my wallet. Second time for my phone. I hit my head against the elevator wall to let my frustration out. Once I reach street level of Hamilton Park subway station I am unable to recollect why I am here. I stand there, trying to focus, trying to remember. I am inside myself but everything is dark. There are no recollecting images of the real world. I shift my concentration from images to time. I try to sense time and space to spark reminiscences of where I could have been before coming here. Memories appear like buildings during a night lightning storm. They are there, I just can't see them. I enter the park as I have always enjoyed walking on gravel and there is nothing else other than the park. I walk forward. My brain is on the lookout for images that could connect me to this place. The park is quiet and lovely at this time of day. Everyone brings their lunches and tries to sunbathe in cold winter sun. I keep moving through the park making this the reason why I came here. When I see Melissa sitting on a bench, my brain gets lit like a high school basketball court. At this moment, and only at this moment, fear sets in. Why could I not remember where I was? This is not normal. What is happening to me? I push myself ahead to engage with Melissa and suppress the questions. She is sitting comfortably, stretched with her right leg over her left one, her hands hidden in her pockets. I go around the bench. Her hair rests on the coarse fabric of her Montgomery coat.

"You scared me!" she says, emphasizing 'me'. Her voice ricochets in my head, disorienting me.

"Sorry." I force a smile whilst I involuntarily try to come to terms with what it felt like not knowing where I was. I find myself to be slightly euphoric for the novelty before a feeling of loss and concern kicks in.

"So how are your women?" Melissa asks whilst putting ChapStick on. I need to adjust my reaction as part of me is still attracted to her.

"Funny you ask." I take a deep breath as I position myself next to her on the bench. I continue speaking with my eyes glued on my New Balance 696 sneakers "It's just very strange. I can't remember any of them. As a matter of fact I couldn't remember why I came here."

"What do you mean?" From the side of my left eye I can see that Melissa has lowered her head and is searching for my eyes.

"When I wake up I can't remember a thing. All I recollect is up to when things are getting interesting. Then I wake up after 4-5 hours recalling the same dream. Actually the weirdest thing happens. Each time the dream picks up from where it left off the previous time. Like a story that unfolds. The best part is that it takes place in a past life and I am an hermaphrodite. I have never had a dream continue from one night to the other, let alone being in a past life and of another sex. You know I got into this to try and cope with a stressful moment but it seems to be making things worse. I feel like I am losing control of my mind." As I talk about it an emotional Deja vu emerges from my last dream. Melissa and I floating as one in the pool. I am unable to make sense of the discrepancy between the closeness I felt in the dream and the distance I experience now. Like a computer my mental process freezes trying to handle something it does not understand. I turn my head and meet Melissa's eyes hoping to find empathy in them. I see a smile which does not reflect the way I am feeling. Rage inflames my chest and morphs into the desire to squeeze my hands around her neck. I look back down at my New Balance again as I try to understand the paradox of desire versus moral.

"That is strange." Melissa accents the 'is'. She then rests her hand on my knee and says "C'mon Vince. It's normal. Other people in the study have reported similar experiences. You just get nervous and you fall into a sort of narcolepsy. It is documented that some men, who suffer from anxiety, will fall asleep during sex."

"Maybe you are right. Maybe you are right." Yes, I want to believe her.

Maybe she is right. I shake my head to get away from the push within.

"I am sure that if you meet this new girl I have found for you, you will have a great time. Think about it and let me know!" Melissa kisses me on the cheek and tells me she has to run back to the lab. I stay on the bench and look onto the small pond in front of me. The water is calm, ripples appear when a small child throws in a pebble. As their circumference increases I remember a quote Zac had tagged me on Facebook: "Just as ripples spread out when a single pebble is dropped into water, the actions of individuals can have far-reaching effects."

# 30

B yron is in town again and has invited me to a
conference. I accept not because I am interested,
but because I hope he might be able to help with
what is going on in my mind.

"How are you, my friend?" Byron greets me with a
beautiful energetic grin and strong half-hug when I get in
his car.

"Quite warm." The car's heater is at maximum level.
I haven't slept all night since I can't stop thinking about the
dream. It feels as if it was injected in me. My mind is on
overdrive, like an immune system that is trying to expel it.

"Not bad, thanks." Byron replies.

"I didn't ask you how you were. I mean, I do care
about how you are, but why do people reply automatically,
expecting that you will ask them how they are?" My
comment comes out unfiltered.

"You mean that I responded automatically to your
reply with 'not bad, thanks,' assuming that you had said
'fine, how are you?' Relax, my man, don't take it so

seriously." Byron reaches for the heater to turn it down. "You are a sensitive man. You can't let it get to you. It's inside that you can change things, not outside." He continues.

"By the way, about those dreams you are having, I have spoken to Dr. Levitt, a psychiatrist who heads the North East Psychiatrist society. He believes what you are experiencing is similar to regression-hypnosis side effects. He told me that it is common to experience daydreaming bouts about a past life right after a session, but not during sleep and without your subconscious being prompted." I am looking at Byron and when he stops I turn away not to appear as terrified as I feel.

He carries on. "Could something have happened during the day that might have caused you to have those dreams? Are you reading about regression? Are you taking any drugs or medication?" Byron's head leans forward to check my facial reaction.

"The only thing I can think of is alcohol. I had a drink every time I met one of those girls."

"Had you been drinking each time you experienced these dreams?" asks Byron.

"Let me think. From the last encounter, the last thing I remember is being on the bed. The woman passed me her drink and then nothing more. Melissa says it could be some sort of sex related anxiety. To deal with the stress of the situation I fall into a sort of narcolepsy."

"You've seen that movie, My Own Private Idaho?" Byron asks.

"No."

"Well, it's easy then, you just have to stop having sex. That's not so hard is it?" Byron nudges me with his elbow, smiling.

"So, is there anything unique about these dreams other than being in another life?" Byron continues.

"I have had recurring dreams before like being a vampire or being swallowed up by a huge wave, but what's remarkable about these dreams is that when they recur the story continues right where it left off the time before." I study Byron's face, hoping to read comprehension.

"The dream always recurs in the same historic period and one particular woman seems to appear."

"Who is this woman? Is she someone you know? Does she remind you of someone? Do you actually know her in real life?" I cannot help but smirk.

"Mother Mary? Miley Cyrus? Michelle Obama?" Byron eyes are wide open and his forehead folds like an accordion.

"Melissa. She is the one who is hooking me up with the women I sleep with. Has she told you about the phone app she developed for the research on digital sexual behavior?"

"She did tell me that she was working on a doctorate, but we never got into what exactly- Byron's hands come together and each finger slithers in between the other- The only thing I can suggest at the moment is that you stop putting yourself in a situation that seems to provoke you stress. Stop seeing these women for a little while. Sometimes, like when we do drugs, our subconscious fights back through our dreams. Here is the address of Dr. Markus Levitt, he is waiting for you to call. Hopefully he can help figuring out the dream," says Byron. I relax my clenched teeth when he hands me the doctor's card.

# 31

D<sub>r. Levitt's</sub> waiting room is much like any other general practitioner's. Cheap chairs, old travel and house magazines his wife subscribes to, and some broken toys his children outgrew long ago. I discovered a secret camaraderie amongst those who meet in a location that suffers from a societal stigma. A porn shop, a drug dealer's house or an underground poker club. You know you shouldn't be there but those you meet in such places feel just like you and offer a mental nod in support of a need that society doesn't accept. A psychiatrist's office should be the same. Those you meet there share a need but are unable to support themselves, let alone someone else.

A teenager with her mother is sitting in front of me. I think of something to chitchat about like Hey kid. Do you feel that rage inside that makes you want to reach a perfect stranger's neck and squeeze the life out of him? Do you feel like there is something stronger inside you that pushes you toward the window ledge?

Outside of this place, where the medical problem is a normal, empirical one there would be no issue in sharing your pain and receiving support for saying: "I feel excruciating pain because the cancer pressures on the spinal cord. I feel a burning sensation as if something were crawling under my skin."

Dr. Levitt is tall and lanky like any basketball player. Byron told me that he had been on his college team. He comes across as a very simple person, although the degrees hanging on his wall communicate otherwise. His simple appearance translates into a very humane demeanor that I have not felt from many doctors before.

"So how are you, Vincent? Byron mentioned you have been having difficulty sleeping. Can you tell me more about it?" He sits with crossed legs, holding his hands in a steeple shape on his knee. Black framed square eyeglasses sit on his prominent nose and his chin is round with a deep cleft.

"I am bit ashamed and I don't know how to phrase this. I have been seeing some women but I seem unable to recall what happens once we are about to get intimate. Then I had a situation where I blacked out," I say.

Dr. Levitt mumbles a "mmmh."

"What's bothering me the most though is a feeling I experienced." I say and look down.

"What is that Vince?"

"I can describe it as an aggressive impulse." I pull myself up as I slowly sink in the leather chair.

"Could you describe it in more detail? How did it start?" Dr. Levitt asks very quietly.

As I hear his voice I feel a sudden relaxation of my limbs and my eyelids drop. I am back in that Roman house. The woman that looks like Melissa is talking to me about Caius and then I see her in front of me in a modern time hotel room. When I open my eyes Dr. Levitt's hand is on my shoulder, calling my name, leaning his buttocks on his desk, right in front of me.

"Vince, take these, they should relax you." He hands me a small cup with some drops in it. I ask him why, what happened, and he tells me:

"You lost consciousness there for a minute or two. How are you feeling?"

I swallow the drops and notice a tremor in my hand. I am not sure if my anxiety is rising because of the sight of my trembling hand or because of my inability to explain the feeling of being absent from myself. I force a smile. My intestines are trying to squeeze fear out of myself.

"I am ok now, thanks." As I hear myself say it, a blanket covers the fire in my chest, confirming that what I am saying is not a formal reply but actual proof that the drops are working. I pass my hand over my forehead and wipe the light sweat on my jeans.

"Is this something you have experienced before?" Dr. Levitt asks as he hands me a tissue.

"Yesterday I was meeting a friend but when I reached the destination of our appointment at first I could not remember why I was there. So, as far as I am aware, this is the second time it happens," I answer, as I wedge my index finger's nail on my bottom teeth.

"Earlier on you also mentioned feeling aggressive? Can you tell me when you started feeling this way?" Dr. Levitt walks back behind his desk and sits on his leather chair. He scribbles on his notebook, then raises his head.

"It's recent. It started over these last few days. I am not sure if it has to do with my frustration at work, with women, with life." I think of Danielle and of how what happened could have had an impact on the way I feel. I decide not to talk about it. "I have just been a pretty peaceful guy all my life and I really don't know what to think of myself now. I tell myself 'oh my god. Is this how a serial killer feels like'?"

"Could you describe this feeling in a bit more detail ?" Dr. Levitt takes off his glasses keeping his stare on me. I don't see a doctor. I see a man who is genuinely interested in me and it scares me.

"I was talking to a friend and I just felt this desire to put my hands around her neck and squeeze the life out of her. Although I know it's not right, the desire is in me. It's like when you have a soar in your mouth and you squeeze it with your teeth. It hurts but it feels good at the same time. That's what I would compare this impulse to. I wonder if this is how a murderer feels before letting go into the desire."

"Vince, we all go through moments like this, maybe in a less intense form. You are experiencing the anger and frustration all at once, as if your moral dyke were tested. It sounds like at times you are overflown by years of frustration and anger. We need you to be patient. I believe that with good therapy you will be able to manage. The right prescription and a good psychotherapist can help you get through this." says Dr. Levitt.

"I hope so. I don't know how to accept myself." I say. "In what way?"

"There is a part of me I don't recognize. I mean the urge I felt was so strong. I have never harmed a fly and there I was needing to feel my hands squeeze the life out of her."

"Can you talk me through the emotions you felt?" Dr. Levitt asks.

"The only thing I can compare it to is sex," I say.

"How does it compare to sex? You also mentioned you have been experiencing some trouble when getting intimate?" Dr. Levitt asks.

"Yes. The emotion is similar to when I am fucking a woman. The need to go deep inside her. To own her."

"Yes. Sex is a great way to express our desires. How about the intimacy problem you mentioned?" Dr. Levitt is hidden behind his clasped hands. I laugh a nervous laugh.

"Well, I have been trying to see a couple of women to get out of my head. You know relax. But the strangest thing happens. I get intimate with these women as far as getting naked and then I fall asleep," I say trying to work out whether in those occasions I might actually be blacking out rather than falling asleep.

"Well Vince. It is a rare condition but we know of some cases of narcolepsy happening during sex. It is usually due to high levels of stress," says Dr. Levitt.

"Tell me about you. What are you doing with your life?" Dr. Levitt continues.

"Mmmm. Not sure where to start. I have been living here for the last 10 years. I am 33. I 've worked in a call center for the last 4 years. I have worked hard to move up the ladder and I used to enjoy my job. I think it has to do with me being shy. You know, it's easier to speak to people over the phone rather than confronting them in person. I have been dating a woman I met in college for about 8 years. She was Korean-American. We used to fight a lot but I wanted to marry her in the end. About 2 years ago she told me that she was leaving me. You know how young love is. You are attached, but then you want to experience more so we started to fall apart. I would go out with my friends and she would stay at home. After the breakup I started to slowly lose interest in my life. She was the port from which I launched my raids. Once she was gone I stayed at sea forgetting why I had set off in the first place." Dr. Levitt looks down at his notebook, then at me, nodding at about 20 seconds intermittence.

"Now I have been focusing mostly on my job. Well, let's say that I let it fill the emptiness in my life. But I don't really know what I am doing there anymore. I wanted to grow, pursue a career and in the beginning I was successful at it.

Now I go to work because I don't want to be home alone. I don't really like the people I work with and I have very few friends."

"What would make you happier in this moment of your life?"

"Good question. I don't know. I thought sex could lift me up, fulfill the void. Sex has always been a reliable source of pleasure for me, be it with someone or alone. But even that does not seem to be working any more. I can't remember anything! I would like to do something worthwhile. You know. Something that makes a difference. Something that give me a reason to be on this earth. Help people maybe."

Dr. Levitt tells me that he will write down the number of a good psychotherapist and a prescription for a 40 mg tablet a day of Cymbalta and Xanax drops to calm me down. I should not take more than 30 drops in a day. For any major problems, should I not feel well, he provides me with the address of St. Martin psychiatric ward. He also gives me the name of a Dr. Fromm who will be able to help, should I not be able to reach him.

# 32

On my way home Jasmine texts me. She's had another fight with her boyfriend.

We've tried to distance ourselves but when an issue arises she calls me. I'll admit I've called her a few times before. Probably mainly as an excuse to have sex. Women seem to be better at a clear cut when they take a final decision. Although I've managed, a few times, to get her to reconsider her stand. Even when she was dating this last guy, I am ashamed to admit. In reply to her text I write I will go visit her.

*"I can't be alone. It will be good to be with her. She makes me feel wanted. I need that."*

*" Oh shut the fuck up you bullshitter. You just want to fuck her. Don't tell me it's not true!"*

*" No! That's not it."*

*" Yes it is. Don't play Mr. Sensitive with me, you loser. All I know is that when we used to have sex it really helped improve our mood. Do you remember when I would come back from work? Depressed as hell and after a good fuck things*

*would get a bit better. We would watch TV in bed. Order pizza in."*

*"God I miss that."*

*"Oh here we go... have you forgotten how you had to start thinking about other women when you were fucking her? You couldn't cum. Is that what you want to do for the rest of your life? You want to live a 'Groundhog' life? Every day the same. Same food, same blowjob, same pussy, for the rest of your life."*

*"Well, this way is getting us far! As if my life has improved so much!" "Whatever man. It's not my problem if you are a fucking loser and can't get a proper bitch. You need to go on these dates like you got some sort of handicap. Are you handicapped Vince?"*

*"Maybe I am. It certainly looks like it. I am unable to be happy. I hate my job. I am alone. And now I feel like I want to decapitate myself. These fucking thoughts are taking over my mind."*

*"I am sorry about that but I told you, you brought this on us. You need to take charge. A directionless captain, welcomes a mutiny."*

A feeling of powerlessness overtakes me. I don't want to use Jasmine. I don't want to go back to what failed, yet I have no one else to turn to. My anger is squeezed between a sense of failure and my loneliness. It appears as a fracture and it breaks me apart.

I take my phone out, wrap it around my hand like a rudimentary weapon and hit myself on the temple. Again. Like a huge wave pain takes over, pushing the unwanted voice into my unconscious. My mental shore absorbs the sense of peace the retreating waves leaves behind.

The internal speaking stops. I am left breathless and resolved by the power to push the thinking away. As I assess the pain and check for blood I am once again pleasantly surprised by the relief and satisfaction my action has brought me.

Before getting to Jasmine I stop by the local liquor store. I need to buffer the pain. My temple is throbbing, releasing endorphins, yet I know the real pain is still to come. When I get to the wine shelves, I see the hard liquors of which I know nothing about. I grab a Sambuca bottle as I have had it before. It is sweet and strong enough to do the job quickly. It is the burning. The fire that burns everything on its gastric path. The fumes that rise up to mist the thoughts. When I get out of the store, I walk quickly toward the car park. As soon as I'm sure no one is around I take the bottle out of the paper bag and take a long swig.

"Hey. Thanks for stopping by. Oh, what did you bring?" Says Jasmine. Her nose is chafed by paper tissues and her eyes are bloodshot. She is wearing an open zipped sweatshirt. I try to look away when I detect her familiar protruding breasts.

She ushers me into her living room. The tv is on and there are tissues all over the coffee table. Once I sit down, she unleashes all the reasons why things aren't working and why Ron, her boyfriend, turned out to be a mistake. I ask if it is ok for me to light up the joint she has prepared and I go on puffing away. I nod, smile and frown methodically to let her know I am listening. She asks if she can get closer so that I can hold her. She then lies down and rests her head on my thigh. After the first puffs I feel as if an invisible cushion is filling out the room. There is no distance between me and the walls. Sound falls on the ground, like water drops. I am liquid. I don't know where I begin or end. The only physical detection is Jasmine's pressure on my leg. I look down at her. She is talking. I quickly lift my head up, overwhelmed by a vertigo. I look ahead and I want to smile. I want to fly away but she's holding me down.

I lift my right hand and place it between her shoulder and her chest. I take another puff to feel her cheek. Slowly I caress her, contouring her features with my index finger. I move from her chin, up to her lips, on to her nose, all they way to her forehead, reaching the scalp. When I look down at her scalp an image of Danielle's nutty hair hacks into my brain. Again I lift my head up to sink back in my groove. I am a sailing boat. Smooth sailing, followed by sudden rock grinding. My hamstrings tense up, pushing me up and with me, Jasmine's head. She stops talking. The TV seems to come back on. I pull my neck up trying to breath more air in.

"I am sorry. I just needed to let this out," says Jasmine.

"Oh, don't worry." I say. I am trying to wedge out Danielle's image. I know I need to reach out. I move my hand on her waist. I keep listening but I concentrate on my hand. On where it wants to go. Where it needs to grab to. Hold on to. It moves higher, it drags on her t-shirt and it reaches her breasts. I know that holding, that gentle squeezing will dissipate the negative charge . I first hover lightly and then land. Jasmine lets me hold on. She knows what I need and she knows that giving me what I need will help her too.

When I am laying naked on the couch, stretched out next to her, I focus on her. I can see her. I remember her weight. Straddling me. I remember sucking on her breasts. I remember not wanting to let go, yet releasing. I am here now. I am focusing on those feelings trying to recollect if any of this happened with Flora, Catalina or Jade.

I want to focus on her smell, her touch, the thought of eating the leftovers. Watching a movie. I am unable to process the disparity between what just happened and the frustration of my last encounters. I tell Jasmine that in the morning I have an early presentation at work and need to go home to rehearse.

She thanks me for stopping by and tells me she is glad to have me in her life.

# 33

In the elevator down from Jasmine's apartment I can't avoid standing in front of the mirror. I search for the man who Jasmine seems to still be in love with. I can see myself but I can't find myself. I so want to find that warmth inside me.

That's what I call love. That replenishing warm air that fills me inside. I try to focus and as I roam inside my chest all I see is darkness. I use Jasmine and our memories like a flare to unearth emotions that are still burning. To create warm air. I stare deeper into my eyes and hear the voices approach.

*"I did feel it, but now I know. I am alone in this. I am the only one who must deal with this."*

*"Yes. People say they are there for you, but no one can get inside your head to fix what is happening." "I do have people who care for me."*

*"Who?"*

*"Jasmine, Zac, Melissa, Byron."*

*"Vince, the loss of consciousness, the panic attacks, the strange dreams. Are these people going to fix those things? I say we go and get some alcohol. That's how you can really help."*

I walk down the street to the first pharmacy to collect the pills Dr. Levitt prescribed. My field of vision seems to be shrinking at every step. A vicious force is compressing my head, my chest. I want to get out of myself, as a surfer takes off his wetsuit. Once the pharmacist hands me the pills I open the container and swallow two of them, without water. I try pushing them down but I feel them stick half way down my throat. I can feel them holding on, sticking to my raw inside. To keep myself from thinking, as soon as I head out I start counting my steps whilst I walk. When I reach 732, my phone starts vibrating in my front pocket. My mouth is dry and my body is slow. I open up the Xanax drops bottle and I pour some in my mouth.

"Hey Vince. Where have you been hiding out? I've got a great girl for you". An internal heat wave startles me. It takes over my entire body. I instinctively grab a hold of the prescription pill container.

"Hey Mel. I am ok, thanks. I am not sure I can do this anymore." "Are you sure? She's really hot and kinky." Melissa sounds genuinely concerned about my rejection.

"I'm just not feeling too well lately. I'm sorry. I think I should take a break. I mean take my profile down."

"Are you ok? No, not really, right? I can tell. Can I come visit you then?" "If you want," I say and let go of the pill container.

When the downstairs buzzer goes off, it startles me. Melissa is already here. I have been in the living room Skyping with Jasmine on my desktop computer to help her decide on a last-minute vacation that might help putting some physical distance between Ron and her. I felt relieved to just listen. It helped me keep my mind off the anxiety, off the thoughts that are coming and going as they please. Jasmine has been talking about her ex whilst random images ranging from my childhood to what the person on the balcony is doing, to a memory of my past life dream kept pulling me their ways. I have been trying to concentrate on what Jasmine was saying to still my mind and focus on the present but the thoughts were carrying me with them like escaping water from a broken dike. Now Melissa is on her way up, and I drag myself to the bedroom to put my jeans on.

"So, how's the man on strike doing?" Melissa never carries a bag. The only time I saw her with a bag was when I followed her to that hotel. She was different then.

"Hey," I would like to say more, but my thoughts are stuck. My brain is engulfed with thoughts.

"I brought you some donuts, chocolate glazed, and some aloe juice. Aloe is really good for your immune system." Melissa places everything on the small table in front of the couch.

I slowly land on the couch, and she follows. She smiles, and as I try to do the same I feel awkward.

"You don't know what you gave up," Melissa says.

I turn my head and smile. I want to be excited but I just can't muster the energy for it.

She sits next to me, offers me a donut and hands me the juice. I keep my hands snug tight between my legs as if to block myself. The urge to strangle her rises from the bottom of my stomach like a geyser. I see it cum through my brain.

I sink my teeth into the donut and wash it down with some juice. I place the glass on the living room table, and when I lean back my hand falls on her leg. I leave it there for contact, yet I need to watch myself. I may lose control and attack her. My brain aches. Not like a headache, but something in between nausea and electrocution. As I quietly sip on my juice, I feel soft kisses moving from my jugular to my ear. A tear slides down my cheek: I realize I am getting further and further away from myself.

# 34

*T*oday Marcus Augustinos will express his decision on whether to grant Caius his freedom . Walking out of his villa, through the garden, I see a lady walking toward me.

"Has Caius been freed?" asks the woman resembling Melissa'.

"The governor has given me his word that he will be freed. There will be a fight between Spiculus and Crixus, the best gladiators this region has seen in the last 10 years. Prior to the fight, Micero will plead for Caius' life . This will ensure a favorable response from the plebs who will be frothing for gladiators' blood in exchange," I reply.

When I wake, the room feels very warm, and Melissa seems to be gone. I wonder whether I fell asleep or had another of my loss of consciousness bouts. I am sweating, but when I reach the heater I realise it is lukewarm. Outside I see snow falling. I want to open the window, but I need to refrain from the urge to jump off. I can't logically explain it. It does not make sense, but part of me desires it. The desire pushes slowly *like a wisdom tooth. For a while you don't know it is there. A life force pushes it forward, ripping your skin, infecting the gum, damaging your nerves to claim its place. When you realise it, it is too late. I drag myself through the room and sit on the sofa's armrest, keeping myself in balance through the tips of my toes. My arms are crossed, and my wrist hurts from the pressure. I sit on the desk nearby where my computer is to get on Skype, hoping to find Byron online. My session with Jasmine seems to be still going on. When she sees me appear in front of the camera she says:*

*"Hey, what the hell were you up to before?"*

*"What do you mean?" I stare at the message window, waiting for a reply.*

*"Who was that woman?" I now realize that the webcam was left on from our earlier conversation.*

*"That was strange. What was it all about? I mean, we were talking, remember? Then you suddenly left so I waited for about two, three minutes. Then I came back on and saw you had left the session open I could see what was happening in your living room. What was that woman doing to you? It seemed like she was going you know.to blow you, but she just laid you on the sofa. You seemed awake but your eyes were closed. Then she sat right in front of you, and started to ask questions. I could not hear very well, but it sounded as if you were talking in your sleep. She was speaking softly. She said something along the lines of 'My voice is just a guide for your*

*journey. It is a warm sunny day. You are very relaxed. A cloud comes down from the sky. The cloud calls on you and you glide on it. Then as you come back down you will find yourself in another life. You are in what was Palestine, during the roman empire. Then she asked if you could find Darius? Caius?"*

*Jasmine continues detailing what she heard, outlining the dream I just woke up from. According to her I voiced the dream to Melissa while she prodded me with questions on Caius' whereabouts and safety. I focus on the words she says avoiding registering their meaning when strung together in a sentence.*

# 35

I open another beer can and feel the tab go deep below my fingernail. I know where it is but I feel no discomfort. I am pacing back and forth between what must be around 6 empty cans which I am not sure how long it has taken me to drink. But, standing in front of the fridge, I know that I have run out. I send a text to Dr. Levitt saying that I need to see him urgently. walk into the living room to get my wallet and slip on my Dr. Martens.

*"Have you thought about it?"*

*"What have I forgotten this time?"*

*"What is the point of all this?"*

*"I am going to see Dr Levitt. He will know what to do."*

*"I told you I was going to take charge. I warned you. I will take charge."*

*"Stop this. Now."*

*"I have the solution to all of this." "And what would that be?" "Look out of the window!"*

*"Ok, now what?" "Now open the door."*

I stop as I am about to grab the balcony door's handle. As I bring my hand back I scream as I hard as I can. When I stop the voice seems to be gone. I swallow 2 Cymbalta pills, then I proceed to pour about 50 drops in a full glass of rum.

When I arrive at Dr. Levitt's office, he is waiting for me at the reception. We greet. He places his hand on my shoulder and asks me how I am doing. He invites me in his office. I tell him what Jasmine saw. I tell him I am starting to feel what I can only describe as severe anxiety. I am barely walking straight.

"Vince, this is similar to a therapeutic procedure I have heard of but thought was abolished. I am not saying this is what is happening, but it certainly sounds like it," Dr. Levitt says as he extracts his glasses from their case. He stares at me, gauging my reaction. I want to look as strong as I usually would, but my brain's barometric pressure is low as fuck.

"Within the field of regression-hypnosis, there is a branch known as past-life regression. It has become quite popular with Brian Weiss, an American psychiatrist who has written the bestseller 'Many lives, many masters.' Within past-life regression hypnosis' techniques there is a controversial approach, called mind-donation."

I am holding onto the chair's armrest. My legs stiffen. I am finding it difficult to breath. Everything is moving too fast, I don't seem to be able to process it all. Dr. Levitt is about to speak, but pauses.

"Vince. Here are some of the drops I gave you last time." Once I swallow, Dr. Levitt walks back to his chair.

"Vince are you with me? Ok. So the story behind Mind Donation is this. An Italian doctor named Frontisi, Ciro Frontisi, developed this technique in the 1940's to cure Dissociative Identity Disorder, at the time known as Multiple Personality Disorder. He believed that when the conscious mind loses control, for a variety of reasons such as post-combat stress disorder for instance, a person's mind becomes weaker and more susceptible to psychiatric conditions like Personality Disorders or Psychosis. A patient starts to hear voices and eventually ends up identifying with them. The voice he hears is thought to be a version of that person in a past life. The voice, or voices, rise up because of an unresolved closure due to an unexpected and violent past life death. The voice disappears when the patient and the voice itself hear that the death has been avoided."

Dr. Levitt takes a sip from his coffee cup and looks at my hands. I glance down and see that they are shaking but I can't feel the movement.

"After World War II, Dr. Frontisi went to the former U.S.S.R. to carry on his studies, but was later on banned by the International Medical Order when it was discovered he was continuing his research on healthy prisoners. His method consisted in using a sane patient as a 'seeker.' Since the sick patient is unable to respond to any sort of regression-therapy, a healthy subject, would be used to go back in time, through what is called 'mind donation'. One man donates his mind to regress in time in order to seek and reconnect with the sick patient's past persona and help it avoid the traumatic death. To find the sick person's past life, or unwanted 'voice', the sick patient joins a seance whilst a medium discovers the moment in time and the location the 'voice' is coming from. The seeker, or healthy patient, under hypnosis, is then regressed by the psychiatrist to the place and time unveiled during the seance to find out how the 'voice' will die. Once the seeker has accessed the era and location of the sick patient's past persona, he attempts to stop the violent death so that the haunting voice will subside in the current patient's pathology, "says Dr. Levitt.

"How can someone go back in time and interfere in someone else's past?"

"Dr. Frontisi believed in Dunne's theory. His close friend, the Irish aeronautical engineer J. W. Dunne, thought that all moments in time are taking place at once, simultaneously. For example, if a cat were to spend its entire life in a box, anyone looking into that box would see the cat's birth, life and death in the same instant - were it not for human consciousness, which only allows us to perceive at a fixed rate.

According to Dunne, whilst human consciousness prevents us from seeing outside of the part of time we are "meant" to look at, whilst we are dreaming we have the ability to traverse all of time without the restriction of consciousness, which translates into a possibility to see our future in dreams. This we then experience in daily life as Deja vu. Henceforth, Dunne believed that we are existing in two parallel states. This requires a complete rethink of the way in which we understand time."

"So is this how I was able to get back in time? Is this why I was asked to avoid Caius' fate?" I ask.

"Yes. The seeker, in this case you, time travels through past life regression to act on the past and avoid the sick patient's death. If he succeeds, he can then reveal his findings to the psychiatrist, who uses the information to communicate with the 'voice' and with the sick patient during the seance. Once the 'voice' recognises the detailed description of the place and event that match his memory l, it disappears from the sick patient's mind.

Dr. Frontisi's research was stopped because his treatment had devastating side effects on the healthy individuals that were used as mind donors. Hypnotizing them without their consent led to a slow fragmentation of the healthy patient's mind. The unconscious material brought into consciousness could no longer be repressed causing complete chaos in the patient's mind. To make it simple, it's as if someone, when you are not home, takes over your house and invites people in for a party. When you get home, you try to convince everyone to leave, but they don't recognize you as the owner who has invited them in, so they ignore you and stay." Dr. Levitt frowns and says "I believe this is what you are experiencing. When I first read about it I found the label of the project ironic. From a label such as Mind Donation you would expect that minds are been given up willingly," Dr Levitt says, keeping his stare on me.

My legs start to frantically open and close. I stare outside the office window looking for a way out of this nightmare.

"But by now they have found a way to deal with this, right?" I say, scratching my itching beard.

Dr. Levitt takes off his glasses and holds them by the temple tips.

"Not that I know of." He turns to me with a faint smile, his mouth closed.

"What if I check into the local psychiatric hospital? They've got to be able to help me!"

Dr. Levitt remains silent.

"You're telling me that I'm fucked. I'm going off of a cliff, and no one can help. You've got to be kidding me!"

"You see, it's like an irreversible decomposition of the mind. Have you ever felt the urge to kick a defenseless kitten or a pregnant lady? It sounds weird, but many people do. When you feel that urge, there is something inside that usually stops you. Right? Through time, with learned behavior, we build a psychological dike that streamlines what needs to become action and what needs to be repressed. What's right and what is wrong according to society's standards. What's happening with you now is that the dike is cracking," says Dr. Levitt.

"What is the point in leading me to insanity and eventual death in order to cure someone else?" I say and think of Danielle laying in front of my building.

"Why wasn't I asked? It's my fucking life! I am not ready to go yet. I don't want to die," I scream. Small drops of saliva hang from my chin. Dr. Levitt gets up and comes close, handing me a paper tissue.

"Vince I'll take you to the university hospital and I'll speak to the head of the psychiatric department. I am sure there are new procedures that can help with this. I'll drive you now."

"I'll go but first I need to do something."

"Vince, it would be advisable for you to be in a safe environment. You are showing high levels of distress." Dr. Levitt seems honestly concerned.

"I am feeling better now Doctor. Really." I get up to prove that I am healthy and grounded. My hands are trying to find each other to create a protection barrier. Dr. Levitt stays seated. I don't want to seat back. I am the client and I can choose what it is best for me.

"You know Vince. It is my responsibility, since you are my client, to take precautions for your wellbeing." Dr. Levitt is holding his pen with the index and thumbs of both hands.

"Dr. Levitt, I swear I am doing much better," I say as I pull my shoulder backward.

"Listen Vince, let me take you to the hospital. I really don't want to coerce you, but it is my legal responsibility to have you assessed."

Dr. Levitt won't let it go.

"Ok, but I did have an appointment."

"I am sure it can wait. Don't you agree?"

As we are getting ready to leave the office, I spot Dr Levitt's mobile on his desk. He has turned around to find my file in his cabinet. I take the phone and hide it in my pocket so that he will not be able to use it once we are outside. Dr Levitt looks for it for about five minutes, then we proceed out to the parking lot. As he gets in his Volvo station I stand outside the car and search into my bag. Once he starts the car I bolt towards the back of the building, up into the garden. I don't mean to keep or throw his cell away. I will drop it off in his mailbox. Be it the last thing I do, I must confront Melissa before I get checked into a hospital.

# 36

The time between the moment I enter the subway and the moment I find myself by Melissa's house is a void. Like time travelling. I am sucked into a vortex of nothingness and I reappear somewhere else. I do know why I am here. I need to find out from Melissa what she has been doing to me and if it is related to what Dr Levitt has explained. Once I reach Melissa's building I decide not to phone her in case she wants to avoid me. I enter the building and walk straight to her apartment. I ring the doorbell first, then I knock. No answer. I climb up a flight of stairs and wait. To try and find out when she will be home I text her asking for a Skype call, as she will be likely to do it from her laptop at home. I start pacing and counting steps to keep my thinking from spiraling out of control. It's like riding a bull. Step 19, I hear someone coming out of the elevator on the floor below. I rush down the stairs and recognise Melissa's silhouette. I quietly stand behind her as she unlocks the door.

"What are you doing here?!" She pulls her hair back in a ponytail as she turns toward me. The keys dangle from the door lock. I want to smile when I hear the ringing of a little bell hanging from the keychain.

"I was in the neighborhood." I can't get myself to tell her more. Hands in my pockets, I move into the living room, scanning her face for signs of deceit.

"I know what you have been doing to me," I say as I first stare outside the window and then slowly turn towards her to read her reaction.

"Yeah, I did not mean to leave your house like that last night. I am going through a hard time and I just needed someone to be close to. The work at the lab is getting to me and I thought I could rely on a friend." She looks down and starts to unbutton her shirt.

"Someone was watching us last night. They saw everything you did to me. My webcam was on." I feel a tear run down my cheek.

"What do you mean?" Melissa asks. She leans over to get close to my neck as if what I just said were irrelevant. I pull back and with my right hand grab the side of her neck. She retreats. I get up and pull her up with me sliding my hand over the front of her neck. When we stand, I am unable to determine her emotions. I detect fear, then, something like defiance. "Vince, I don't know what this is about but I am sure you have your reasons.

Out of all people I would never want to hurt you. I am actually trying to help you," says Melissa, staring into my eyes. I am sinking into her stare. Then, I feel a sharp pain on my ear. Whilst getting up Melissa had grabbed a glass with her left hand. I instinctively let go of my hold and Melissa runs for the door. I chase her and pull her by her pointy tail. I pin her down to the floor and sit on her chest, extend her arms above her head and press them down with my knees. My crotch in her face.

"Why me? Why did you have to do this to me?" I can feel the vein in my forehead swell. Small quantities of saliva drop on her face as my teeth clench. She, the reality creator. I, the small child caught in it.

"Answer me!" Tears follow my saliva as I scream into an expressionless face. I grab her neck with my right hand. My left hand tightens into a fist. I find a precum pleasure in the thought of crushing her septum. Of seeing thick burgundy blood trickle on her rosy cheeks. I open my hand to reason and pull her back up onto the couch. I keep my hold on her neck.

"You were pointed out by one of my patients as someone who needed a cause. Someone without a family, single, and without any real responsibilities, someone who needed a reason to be. We figured you would approve of our cause."

"Wait. Who told you that? Who came up with this description?" I ask.

"Todd," she utters. She seems out of breath. I look and stare at my fingers, sunk deep into her side neck muscles. I discover pleasure in the sensation of penetrating between her fibers. It turns into obfuscating exhilaration that takes over all other senses. My nails turn pale as I exert increasing.

"Todd? What does he know about me?" I say.

"I can't breathe Vince. Please let go." I relieve some pressure but keep her under my control.

"You guys are co-workers and you went on a trip with him, didn't' you? He told me how blazè you are about life. How you feel that god is missing in your life and how you wished to find a way to do something that matters. So I thought you would have welcomed this opportunity."

"How and when did this get started?" I ask.

"He introduced my name into your phone call list at work".

"So you were expecting my call that day? You went along throughout the call? Our dates, the university research, the offers to meet other women, it was all planned ahead? Why not just ask me if I would be willing to help?"

"We have tried before to reach out directly to people like you. But you seem to be caught in this warp. You see that your life is not going anywhere. At first you feel depressed, then frustrated and finally suicidal. But if someone asks you 'would you give your life to save someone else?' your survival system kicks in overriding the suicidal instinct. The person asking for your life becomes a threat. When people desire to die and are asked to donate their life to another purpose, it is no longer felt as a suicide, or as an act of defiance towards this reality. In essence, people kill themselves because they want to s believe they are in control. They don't want to admit to what they can't accept, solve or achieve. So to cut a long story short, when we approached suicidal cases they wouldn't comply as they felt they wanted to send quite an opposite message to the world: 'This reality has taken everything from me but I won't let it take the most important thing of all. My life'. It's a paradox, a lose-lose game.

What we are asking for is rather different. We are asking for the ultimate sacrifice, for an act of love, not for one of selfishness. We are asking to give a life in order to save one. Suicide bombers come to believe that their action is an act of ultimate love towards themselves and towards those around them. This of course would be the ideal attitude, but it takes too long to convince people. Our cause is not a millenary religion. We can't afford to wait for willing martyrs, " says Melissa.

"How did you get those women to sleep with me?" I ask.

"They're our university patients or they are somewhat connected to a patient. Each of those women has been briefed to connect with the 'seeker' and to create the right environment for the mind donation to take place. They knew you were their way out of suffering."

"What about the dreams? Did you have anything to do with those? What were you doing in my dreams? Who is Caius?" I ask.

"Caius is a past life of an African-American woman suffering from schizophrenia. A past life that ended in a violent manner. It has surfaced in her mind in the form of auditory hallucinations, determining her schizoid condition. But if we rewrite its story and avoid the violent death it has no reason to come back in this life. That's why you had to go and avoid Caius' death. Then, in my one-to-one patient therapy, with the absence of the obstructing voice, the patient will become aware of the erroneous identification. "She goes silent. Then pleads: "Vince, we need you to save Caius. Please don't destroy everything we have done."

. "The black couple back in the hotel, is that what they were talking about?" "How do you know about them?" Melissa asks.

"I followed you."

"Why?"

"Because I thought you cared about me? I thought there could be something between us. I needed to feel close to you, so I came by your house. Then when I was there waiting for you I saw you come out of the building and you looked like someone I did not know. I was intrigued by this person that seemed to be you but did not look like the you I met. So I started to follow you. Being close to you was enough for me. When you are lonely you learn to take what you can and that might mean to even just be at a certain distance. Watching is safe when you don't have what it takes or what is wanted."

"Please let go of my neck. I can help you feel better if you only allow me to. Don't throw all the work we have done away. We need to save Caius." Melissa insists.

I push myself to decrease the pressure I'm exerting on her neck and drag her along by her hair into the studio.

"How were you able to hypnotize me without me even knowing it?!".

"Rohypnol & Midazolam."

"Rohypnol the date drug?"

"Yes. By combining the two drugs we can achieve patient's' cooperation as well as amnesia."

"Motherfucker. That is why I would wake up in the morning with my head all fucked up and not remembering a thing!"

"Am I the only one in this program? Who else are you doing this to? Tell me and I might not choke you on the spot."

"What does it matter to you?" Melissa asks.

I grab her by the neck, open the balcony window and push her toward the rail.

"Give me the names of all the people you are doing this to or I swear I'll throw you over." I hiss between my teeth.

A faint smile appears on Melissa's face and she tells me:

"Ok, stay calm. Let me get to my computer and I'll give you the program roster."

She sits at the computer, prints a file containing about 20 names and hands it over. I scan through the list and find my name amongst the last. Something causes me sudden alarm. I look at the list again. The third name on it is Danielle Boban.

"This woman here. Danielle Boban. What can you tell me about her?" I say as my hands constrict the back of her neck.

"Who? Danielle? What do you want to know?"

"Yes, her. She approached me on the street. She told me someone was looking for me. She wasn't able to tell me who it was before jumping off my building."

As Melissa says, "God that sounds terrible," she reaches for the scissors laying on the desk. I instinctively retreat and punch her straight in the back of the head. The scissors drop off her hand and she falls forward onto the desk, unconscious. I shake her, but she remains still.

*Micero stands next to the governor. He begins his speech by thanking Jove, the god of thunder for allowing the games to take place and Opi's good disposition for this year's harvest. Today two of the mightiest gladiators from the school of Neapolis will fight to death. At the end of his introductory speech he signals to the guards down in the arena to bring Caius out of the holding cage.*

*"Romans, the man in front of you is guilty of murder. c Let's call it weakness of the mind. Our last war campaign has shown us that great men can taint themselves of despicable acts. Fear and loss of judgement can attack the mightiest heroes in these difficult times. After the many casualties we suffered during our last confrontation with King Euphrates, should we kill another of our own? The gods are with us today and enough blood has been shed to appease them during the last war. Let's show the gods the valour and clemency of roman people. Should*

the punishment for Caius' crime be decapitation or exile to roam in shame forever?" As Micero pronounces his last words, Caius is lead out of the arena to be judged at the end of the gladiators' battle. Prixus the Gaul and Vetraites the Thrace are ushered in the coliseum to select their weapons of choice. Prixus, fighting in the murmillones style, wields a short sword, a rectangle shield, a helmet, arm guards, and shin guards. Vetraites, a hoplomachi, wears a helmet bearing a griffin, holds a spear and a small round shield, leg wrappings and shin guards.

Insults toward Caius are faint. The fans are ecstatic about the presence of 2 of the greatest stars in the game and seem to be annoyed by Caius' case. Micero's plan to use the gladiator's fight to sway the fans decision over Caius' crime seems to be working. When the fighters go back to their holding pen, the crowd quiets whilst the energy on the stands is that of a humming sound. As part of the pre-fight entertainment king Euphrates prisoners are also brought into the arena. The soldiers push them to circle the arena as the crowd spits and urinates on them. When the spoils of war are ushered out of the arena, Micero stands again.

"Brothers and sisters, we will need you to take a stand on Caius. Caius failed our trust but does he deserve death or exile? We have just seen the faces of our real enemy. By empowerment of the Roman Senate, by the end of the fight you will show us your thumbs in favor or against Caius."

It is hard to make out what the consensus is from the screams.

The battle between Prixus and Vetraites begins with both fighters circling at an arm's length distance. The exchange of attacks is swift and repetitious. The men know each other's style perfectly well and dance with one another to enjoy their last breaths. Belonging to the same training school they have done this many times and enjoy the ease and familiarity of the movements. Each awaits for the other to begin the mortal attack. When the fight has gone on for 15 minutes, Vetraites lunges in with his spear closer to Prixus right shin where his shield cannot protect him. Prixus swerves his sword to deviate the incoming pole and leans forward. Vetraites raises his shield and hits him below his chin. Prixus falls on the ground motionless. With his spear Vetraites nudges his opponent who, slightly stunned, quickly gets up shaking his head and hitting his gladius over his shield. The crowd is split between desiring Prixus' death and wanting for the entertainment to continue. Vetraites stands at a distance to protect himself from Prixus' short sword's flexible range. He keeps poking the Gaul waiting for an opening. Prixus awaits for a longer lunge by Vetraites to let go of his shield. With his free hand he grabs on to the spear. He pulls Vetraites closer and with his sword swings from the top to the right side of Prixus' abdomen. The Gaul intersects the attack with his shield and both gladiators start wrestling, body to body, looking for an opening into each other's flesh.

*Vetraites, needing a longer range to use his lance, is at greater risk. To gain distance, he hits his opponent in the face with his helmet. Prixus is stunned when the edge of Vetraites galea smashes on his nose bridge. He lets go of the lance and as he retreats he brings his shield up to protect himself and focus on his pain. As the men stand at about 5 meters apart, the battle to the death has begun.*

*Adrenalin is pumping in Prixus' bloodstream to counter the blow. Vetraites' heart rate is slowing as he has regained a safe distance from Prixus' sword. Both fighters are slowly moving in a circle to understand how to deliver the best attack. Vetraites, with the advantage of distance, begins to swing his spear circularly at head and feet level. Prixus lets go of his shield handle and holds the metal discus forward by the brim. When the spear hits the shield Prixus moves forward so that the spear head slides into the shield's handle making it impossible for Vetraites to pull the spear away. Prixus pushes the shield down to the ground and Vetraites lets go of the spear. Prixus comes forward to strike with his gladius as Vetraites, weaponless, protects himself with the shield in the left hand and his helmet on the right. Prixus is now focused on pushing Vetraites away from the spear toward the arena wall. He begins swinging to the right side were Vetraites is holding his helmet. At the third strike Vetraites hands are bleeding and the helmet falls on the sand. At this point, the Thrace knows that his faith is sealed. To show his courage and pride he drops his shield and calls on his god Bassareus as he runs toward Prixus. The Gaul brings his shield forward to sustain the last incoming attack. When Vetraites hits against the shield, Prixus shoulder recoils whilst his sword penetrates Vetraites' abdomen and exits through his lower back.*

*The crowd cannot see Vetraites smiling as he slowly falls on the sand. The survivor stands above the defeated with his sword up in the sky waiting for Marcus Augustino's decision. Give the Thrace another fight or end his life. The Governor rises from his throne and looks around the arena to wait for the crowd decision before his final call. The plebs almost uniformly turn their thumb down. Marcus Augustinos follows by slowly extending his left arm before him. The crowd goes quiet when the governor twists his thumb down. Then, it goes wild and intonates the word 'head, head, head.'*

When I gain consciousness again, I am sitting on the ground next to Melissa. It feels like child's play. I feel abandoned as my provider stays silent leaving me in neglect. I bring my hand to my head and squeeze my temples.

I am aware that this time, similarly to what happened when I was with Dr. Levitt, I have lost consciousness without any forced hypnosis. I try to breathe slowly, deeply. I place my palms on the floor to seek connection, support. I stand up, reach for my coat and swallow a couple of pills. I feel as if my gut had been pierced through and flames of anxiety were bursting out of it.

# 37

Next day I am at St. Francis Hospital, 4th floor, room 7D. This is where Zac has been brought. I need to see him before it is too late for the both of us. The Hospital is where we are born and where we die, yet we go through life avoiding the place. We would probably be happier if we came back periodically to be reminded of how easily life comes and goes.

Zac's head is tilted on his shoulder, the TV is on, and there is a newspaper on the bed. I turn around and quickly get out of the room. I head toward the bathroom next door. I lock the door and stand in front of the mirror.

*"You don't have the balls to say goodbye to your friend?"*

*"I am a coward."*

*"What about us? Aren't we dying?"*

*"We deserve to die. He does not."*

I place my hands on the sink to feel assurance. I open the faucet and splash my face. I let the cold water run and wet my hand to then bring it to the base of my neck. I need to cool the stream of matter running from and to my brain. My facial numbness hums like the neon light just above the sink. It's monotone, tense, pure energy that turns to fire at the touch of human flesh. My head is an incandescent bulb. My brain, tungsten filament losing resistance, unable to contain the heat before explosion. I walk back into the room and roll up a magazine. It helps keep my hands steady.

"You look like shit," Zac says, surprising me as his eyes are still closed. His arm, where the intravenous needle is inserted, is full of bruises. Behind him, a white screen seems to be connected to him through a 1-inch tube coming out of his back. At witching spreads from my hands to my legs, so I sit and try to smile.

"You know, I am not afraid of dying anymore," says Zachary as I sit closer, on the edge of the bed.

"I don't believe it. You, Mr. Hypochondriac, are not afraid of fear number 1?" I say. The humming sound continues. The bed light above Zac's head echoes like a sonar. I turn my right ear toward him to ease his sound into my eardrum.

"I'm not. Seriously. I have been practicing and it ain't too bad," Zachary says, keeping his eyes down.

"You have been practicing?" I ask.

"My lungs are collapsing and when I don't get enough oxygen it feels like I'm dying. It lasts enough time for me to realize what it will be like at the end. I figure that death is not really the problem, but the desperation to stay attached to this body, to this life. Maybe because attachment to life stems from not knowing the outcome. Now that I know it is really happening, it does not feel so scary anymore. When I feel like I am about to go, I realize it is not fear I am experiencing, but a resistance to unwanted change because I have not accepted death. Anything I can't accept is painful and similar to a small or big death. Can you pass me that water, please?"

"Makes sense." My eyes hurt. I want to cry, but I don't seem to be able to. Images of my dreams appear in my reflection in the window glass. I take my house key and push it hard on the back of my left hand. The pain pushes me out of myself, into the room.

I stay with Zac until the nurse asks me to leave. He looks at me, he does not say a word, but with a faint smile he tells me the following:

"Vince, it's not easy to go, but you gotta take what life gives you. I've loved you like a brother. Hold on. I still love you and will always love you like a brother. I don't know what happens once that last moment comes, but all I know is that I need to be grateful because this is the only way to accept this. At times I get very angry for not having done this or that. But I realized there is beauty in this situation. What's ahead is clear as it has never been before. It's like being in a corner and looking with your back to the wall. You can only go in one direction. Forward. Thank you for sharing this ride with me. Thanks to all those with whom I have shared the bus, laid on the beach, all those unknown people that have filled my everyday experience in this world. Now I either stand here or move forward."

On the way down, in the elevator, I look at the mark I made on my hand with the house key. I see blood, burgundy blood. I lick it off. I see a cigarette burn right above it and remember Zac dropping the hot ash on me. I was 19. These two girls had invited us over and we had been drinking. I was not going to show pain. I was tough.

# 38

The wind is blowing on my face. It's cold, and I can't stop thinking about the time when Zachary and I first met. The excitement of feeling love before emasculating it for a woman. The purest kind. Untainted by sexual desire or familiar circumstance. Just pure soul reflection. All recollections fade away, blasted by a panic siren taking over my thinking. An ambulance passes by crystallizing the feeling from within to a deafening sound. I look down to my hand and see the cigarette I have lit burning my skin. I let it go and slowly or at least this is how everything feels like, I put my hand in my pocket and find the list I took off Melissa. I think of Dr Levitts' words about 'an irreversible process of mental decomposition' and resolve that the last thing I can do is to find one of the people, that like me, were targeted by Melissa. I go through the list and recognize Chiswick Road.

Tom Phelps

19 D Eldorado Park

35 Chiswick Road

As I raise my gaze from the paper I find myself in front of a store window staring at a silhouette. I hear a small dog barking at me and see what must be its reflection in the window next to the silhouette. I step closer to the window in order to understand if the reflection is mine. As I get closer, next to the dog's silhouette, appears that of a man.

"Hey Vince." The voice is monotone and familiar. I drag my eyes away from the store window and understand why it sounded so familiar.

"Todd?" I say, wondering if this is the same man that was part of my everyday life. He appears different, standing erect and refined.

"Hi Vince. I heard you went to visit Melissa. Can we talk before you do anything illogical?" His appearance makes him the Todd I know, but not his voice and demeanor. They feel distant and inquisitive.

"What do you mean illogical? I thought I knew what that word meant but I am not sure now. What do you know about me and Melissa?" I ask.

Todd invites me for a quick coffee at the nearby Starbucks. I follow him and sit at a table with my shoulders to the wall. I keep my jacket on and my right hand in the pocket where the list is. I touch it not to lose focus on what I need to do. When Todd comes back with the latte I don't touch it. He sits and he keeps his Chihuahua on his lap, which I find disturbing. It, the dog, looks at me as if knowing how I feel. As if it was me in another life.

"Vince. Remember the trip we took together? During the talks we had you practically said you are a man who has no real direction in life. You sounded lost, with a desperate need to find a reason to your life. We gave your life a reason, a chance to make a difference. So many people talk about putting their life toward a good cause, but never do anything about it. As we were speaking over lunch about that colleague of ours who committed suicide you agreed to the right to forgo life if it felt it was the right thing to do We just nudged you because we actually believe that if this had been a legalized therapy, you would have willingly offered yourself. You have a kind soul. What you did has saved a life and you should be proud of yourself."

My eyes are watery as an emotion is being squeezed out of my self, not by myself. I feel my lips extend sideways against my will. When I rest my clenched hands on the table, knuckle to knuckle, Todd reaches out and places his right hand over them.

"She saved me, Vince." He shifts the dog on the chair next to him and moves forward across the table.

"I remember seeing you at work. Dragging yourself to get anything done, a walking zombie. You were looking for a reason, any reason that made your existence worthwhile.

We knew that this would be something that could make you feel you have accomplished something good in life. I have seen it before. It's hard at first to accept that you weren't the one to decide, but in due time you will accept it. Think of Jesus. He didn't know that he was the son of god and that to save us he had to give his own life."

"So it works?" I ask, repressing my anger.

"Yes it does, and I am living proof. I was diagnosed with schizoaffective disorder. People with this illness present symptoms of both schizophrenia and a mood disorder, such as depression or bipolar disorder. I had tried everything. During my teenage years I was in and out of institutions, until I met Melissa. I was studying Psychology at University and went to a conference where I was so intrigued by regression hypnosis that I wrote to Melissa asking for more information on the topic. When we met in person I told her about my condition and she got me involved in the Mind Donor project," Todd explains.

Unfortunately one of us needs to suffer so that many of us can survive. You have helped the research move on. Many will survive because of what we learned from you." Todd smiles with compassion and squeezes my hands.

"You have no idea what is happening in my head right now." I catch myself almost smiling. I, Vince Zemolo, have done something to be proud of in this life. It is pride that awakens the anger lingering on me like bad breath. I don't smell it but I recognize it in the distancing of Tod's upper body. My hand finds my house key in my pocket. I feel an urge to slowly lodge it in his left eye. I can picture it turn in his socket as if to dislodge the reason why mankind is just not what you see.

"This is why I am here. You can get help at the university hospital. Dr. Fromm has developed a drug cocktail that can stop the uncontrolled thinking and panic that you are experiencing. Go there. They are waiting for you," says Todd.

# 39

I have asked Dr Levitt to meet me by the entrance of the university hospital. I am trying really hard to stay with myself. In waves, I am overtaken by an urge to climb a building's top and end this agony. It's a drive I have never felt before. 100 times stronger then when you are hungry, horny or coked up. All senses shut down, my heart races and my sense of self is squeezed out of me by this internal force. I can't breathe and my nerves are electrocuting the back of my head, inside.

"Dr Levitt, I don't know how much longer I can resist," I tell him as I move backward to find support from the wall. My right knee gives into a tremor.

"Take a deep breath, we're here now. There are some of the best physicians in the country in this hospital." Dr Levitt frowns as he looks away from me. He walks inside the hospital hall and speaks to someone at the check-in desk. Then, he comes back and tells me to follow the nurse who escorts me on the second floor of the psychiatric ward. Dr Levitt tells me to stay with my breathing. He will be back as soon as they check me in. The nurse ushers me into a room and informs me that Dr. Fromm will arrive soon.

"Dr. Fromm will be right with you. If you need help push this button and someone from the ward will answer." As I sit on the desk chair I see the nurse walk away and hear the turning of the lock after she has closed the door. I get up, walk towards the door and confirm that I am locked in. I try the knob again and the door stands still. I message Dr Levitt telling him I have been locked in and he replies that it is just part of the process and not to worry. I sit down, put my hands in my pocket and touch the paper where Melissa's list is on. I realize I can't wait here from what maybe the rest of my short conscious life. The destructive force within me comes back with greater intensity and pushes me towards the window. I am only on the second floor so I try to sit myself back down, then I start pacing, my mind along with me.

*"Look what you got ourselves into, you fuck!"*

*"I don't want to die."*

*"Oh, now we are crying. Are we? How about all the time you wasted when you could have made something of yourself? If you had been good at something we wouldn't be here. You would be with a nice girl, maybe a family, who knows, a child."*

MICHELE SCARANO

*"I tried, I really did. It's not my fault. It was you. You messed me up. T."*

*"Shut the fuck up. You are an adult man. Aren't you ashamed of yourself? You know how many people had it worse than you and made their life worth something? I raised you to be a man not a wining child."*

*"You are right, I am weak. It's genetics. I have probably survived too long. If I were in the wild I would have been dead long ago."*

*"You should have listened to me. I have been watching you for a long time. Since you were 6. Remember? You were trying to learn that poem for school. I grabbed you by the head and smashed it against the wall because you couldn't remember the lines. I knew one day I would have to come back to be in charge of things. Then, it was different. Yes, everyone used to beat you for being an active child. Your father, when he was not travelling, your grandfather, your older cousin. I needed their help. You were unmanageable. I know you trusted me. You thought I was on your side. When I kept hitting your head against the wall, I was trying to rattle the bad out of you."*

*"I wasn't very good in school. Yes. I wished I had more attention from you ."*

*"Listen to yourself whine like a baby. You are just the way you are and if you made it up to today is because I took things into my own hands."*

*"Wait, I took things into my own hands!"*

*"I was the one that evened things up. I was the one giving you some sort of pride so that you could continue believing you weren't entirely a waste of oxygen. Remember when you threw that brick through the window because you were grounded for failing 4th grade? Scratching your math's professor's new BMW with a razor blade? You think you would have lasted long with all that humiliation? Someone had to retaliate."*

*"I did it because I was angry. They didn't' understand that I was trying. It was as if I could not sit still. There was something stirring inside me. A fire in my chest burning me from the inside."*

*"Yes, right. That is what you think it was. It was me. I was helping you survive. Stand up to the shit the world was putting you through. You see, now I am back because once again you are unable to take things in your own hands. You could actually learn a thing or two from Melissa."*

# 40

From the small anti shatter glass window carved in the door, Dr. Levitt appears to be speaking to a female doctor whose hair dangles familiarly on her white coat. Fear spreads like a house fire from the center of my chest, biceps, forearms, finger tips down to the bladder, inner thigh and calves. I keep staring through the window. All muscles contract painfully when the doctor faces my direction. Melissa. Dr. Melissa Fromm. My fingers perched on the glass border slip into free fall and I move away from the door backtracking slowly. The window seems to open only slightly at a 30 degree angle. I try to force it open wider but I am unable to. I look around for a way out. I take small steps toward the wall and slide down with my knees to my chest. I wrap my arms around my legs and start rocking back and forth.

I glance up to determine where the music is coming from. I look at the top corners of the room and I see no speakers.

A recessed ceiling light is right above me. The kind that fit within the ceiling cavity. I align myself to look just below it. A sudden realization forms into a thought. My eyes widen and my back contracts. Shivers ripple on my arms. I can see from its spherical shape and dark center that it is more than just a light. I recoil from the wall, pull my legs tighter to my chest and tie them with my arms. I look forward. I am too frightened to lift my head up. From far away regions comes the belief that it can't be true. I unlock my arms around my knees and lean against the wall. I rest my head on my right arm to feel warmth. Human warmth. Sound halved by ear pressure on the bicep. My back starts to extend as the outside seems to fade. I raise my left arm to press on my ear. It dangles over my head.

I keep the position for about a minute and then accept that it is not an option. I let my arm slide down on my knee. When I look up again my third eye feels a presence. I can't locate it at first. It's a primordial instinct. I look around but I can't see it. I look up and again, that light bulb. Or so they want me to believe.

It's a camera. My third eye knows.

I slowly get up. I get as far away from the light bulb as I can and sit outside its peripheral view. Then, I spot another one. Not directly above me, but it can still see me. My legs are extended and crossed. My hands are tight in between them. I try to swallow but I find it hard. I keep hoping that belief will turn into doubt but it overtakes me. It's not a mere thought I am dealing with. It's overwhelming fear, pressing me against the wall. The fine line between believing and not believing what i feel real. It's the moment when your foot is leaving the ledge. Part of me is still touching the ground, but it's too late. The weight of fear has already pushed me into panic. You don't reason with a motherfucking tsunami. You run. My head is twisting away from the rest of my convulsing body. I am breaking in two. A hole opens in my chest like a portal. My soul is sucked away towards the camera that has morphed into a probe. I scream as loud as I can but no sound comes out. Just twisting nerves and spasmodic muscles. The probe is pulling my heart away.

Dr. Fromm enters my view and leans toward me. I look down and recognize those black boots. Knee high. Her mouth is moving but I can't hear what she saying. I grab onto her white coat and try to hold on. The needle enters my neck and I see myself float toward the ceiling.

I look up. I turn my eyes ahead and see a window and a metal bed rail. My pupil turns to the right, meeting a desk on which is a tray with a dish in it. Its steam gradually fights its way up into emptiness. I try to add consciousness with surrounding but l can't go further. My mental eyelid is too heavy. My mind falls dark. I linger in presence. I bring my eyes back to the plate's condensing air. Like me, it moves.

Stillness. Movement. I look down toward the window and a bulge appears below the metal rail. I watch it. It rests still. I look out toward the window. The color through it is similar to the one of the ceiling, but its texture is softer. I catch a movement from the corner of my eye. The bulge has moved and with it my mind. A sharp pain tells me there is more of me below the blanket. I want to bring the stinging pain towards me but I register opposition. I try to pull but I can't. I am aware of an initial movement, but it comes to a halt. I pull harder and feel the restraint coming from the side railing where a strap is tensed.

I go back to ceiling and there, once again, I try to jump from image and sensation to me. Ceiling, restriction, hunger, pain. I try to bring them together. I find myself doing it over and over again. I switch their order, nothing more. Then, I add window, rail, grayness. Separate, indistinct images. I continue adding all I see, stacking things on top of each other to reach my mind. When I forget one item, I start stacking all over again.

I hear a sound coming from my right side and I turn my head slightly. A mélange of noises approaches. A white coat, open on a white sweater and black trousers. The body comes closer." How are you feeling, Vince?" Where is the voice coming from? I can only make out a pair of hands and a syringe with some yellow fluid in it. Then, it is a skin prick on my arm.

I am in a wheelchair. They are pushing me through halls. My left thumb, wrapped in a bandage, is resting on my lap. I feel a slight numb pain but I can't tell why it is there. The air is far too cold for what I am wearing. The room I am brought in is much bigger than the one I am sleeping in. There are more people in it. Some walking, other sitting. Most of them are huddled around a coffee machine. Others come in and out from outside. I can feel the draft. I bring my hands to the wheel and start pushing myself. It is quiet yet everyone is making busy noises. Abrupt movements, crushing cups, slamming fists against the coffee machine, fast newspaper page turning. Everything is familiar, yet a t burn mark on my arm asks me to withdraw into an empty room. My memory. I bring my hand to the burn mark and press to see if a recollection will spring out. I recognize a face. Jade. She is sitting on the bench by the wall on the opposite side of the coffee machine. She is small, her hair is black, straight and it frames her harmonic face. I smile at her but she is focused on something behind me. I am in her way. I push the wheel to place myself out of her trajectory. I look toward her target and I see the bare white wall. I want to speak but I know that waking up the third eye has repercussions. Jade's bracelet slides from her wrist to her forearm as she repeatedly passes her hand over face.

I remain in the center of the room. In front of me a door leads to an outside area. I watch, that is all I will do. The third eye has a way I cannot understand. It shows me it has power over anything. When it awakes and the eyelid is wide open everything becomes unpredictable. It gives me the power to see what I can't see. Hear what I can't hear. Be where I can't be. When I catch myself raise up to it with a thought stacked over another, gifts collected for offering to the sleeping dragon, I shake myself causing any train of thought to derail. Because the third eye giveth and taketh away. This is why I move quietly, speak insufficiently and most importantly, think inconsequentially.

My chair starts moving toward the outside door. I raise my eyes up as if to find out whether I have inadvertently awakened the one. I can hear a humming coming from behind. I turn slightly and see big dark hands wrapped around the push handles.

When we are outside the man lays a blanket on my legs and asks me if I want a cigarette. I nod.

"You know Vince, every time I smoke a cigarette, I feel I have accomplished something." He opens up the paper, grubs some tobacco in between those thick indexes and thumbs and layers it across it. Then he takes the filter out of its tin can and juxtaposes it to the tobacco. He gently folds the paper and squeezes the tobacco for it to take shape before rolling the paper. Carefully, he licks the glued edge to a tight roll. He does it once for me and once for himself.

"I didn't use to smoke before coming here. I really could not understand the need." When he realises that I am sucking on air, he takes out his silver Zippo lighter and lights my cigarette up again. I stare at the engraving on the lighter but can't make out what it reads.

He opens his hand and brings it closer to me.

"Oh yes, it's my friend Todd's. Well, he is not a real friend but he lends it to me. He shouldn't really, but he knows I am safe." It reads 'Mother Mary loved you this much.'

"You know, as I was saying, when I got here and started to feel better I had another disease to deal with. Time. Each second was a reminder of how I was unable to live. I was unable to stand what others out there seem to do so well. Living. So here is my crutch- the dark handed man takes the rollie in between his thumb and index and brings it up to revel at its magic - Some say that smoking is a slow suicide. You sabotage the most essential human act. Breathing. When you are as desperate as we are who gives a fuck. Right? - he chuckles as he hits the ground with the front of his right shoe - In my other life I was busy all day, running around, making multi million dollars deals and feeling like I never had enough time. " He sees that my cigarette isn't lit and lights it up once again. He takes a deep inhale, closes his eyes and stays silent trying to hold on to the drag as long as possible. His eyes look into the cloudy smoke as shaky airplane headlights trying to peer into an incoming turbulence.

"You know it's that burning in the chest that tells me I am still alive. Now cigarettes are my units of time. They give me a reason to get up every morning. It's as if I was back to work. I plan, you see. I know the tobacco deliveries and order only at the beginning of the month. I have researched which type of rolling paper is less chemically treated and only use French Zig Zag filters. You know, there are 2 kinds of rolling papers. Slow and fast combustion, to help the burning of two types of tobacco. You have humid and dry tobacco. For the humid tobacco you want to use papers that are white, thick and porous, as they will burn faster and help the burning of the humid tobacco. There are this small wings that help the catching of fire even when you are not inhaling. Then for the dry tobacco you want papers that are thin and transparent. These are good for fast burning dry tobacco as they burn slower or actually go off when you are not inhaling. That's why your cigarette keeps on going off." He smiles, flicks the cigarette butt and squeezes his cheeks with his hand. He then takes his shoe off and pulls out a list with timings for each cigarette and tells me that tonight he will skip the 11pm one since he has offered me one.

Once we are done with our cigarettes he pushes me back inside the activities room. There, he greets a man dressed in white canvas trousers, white long sleeve t-shirt and black Timberland-like boots. Before saying goodbye he hands the zippo lighter to him.

"Vince, remember what I always tell you. Breathe. It's the only currency eft to us," says the dark handsome man. His face is round and hairless, like that of a child.

The Zippo man pushes me back through the halls from which I came in. We stop by an office door. He knocks and I am led in.

The room has a long table where, on one side, I see Dr. Fromm and Dr. Levitt. They tell me that I am looking good and that judging by the papers in front of them, the relapse should be behind us. I smile. I am happy but I need to stay calm. Any vibration could awaken the dragon.

"Vince we want to hear from you. How do you think it's going?" Dr. Fromm asks. She glances at the tight dressing on my left thumb. I wish I could explain my fear but I know they would not understand.

"Ok." I look up imploringly. I take off my gold, round, thin glasses and scratch my beard.

"How is your thumb feeling?" Dr. Levitt leans his body over the table.

I look down and become aware of the throbbing that seemed to have been dormant until I acknowledged it. I smile, look into his eyes and then down in between my feet and through the darkness below the table.

"Now, I would like for you to look at these images and tell me what you see. This is called the Rorschach test. It is employed when patients have difficulty expressing themselves. We understand you are having trouble speaking and we need to know what is happening to help you help yourself" Dr Fromm takes out a deck of strange abstract images. She looks at Dr. Levitt as if to check whether he wants to add anything. He shakes his head.. He reminds me of a parent looking at his child. Waiting for it to take the first step.

Some of the cards are entirely black, others colored. They make me think of watercolors drawings in a primary school. I feel my eyes close. I want them to leave me alone, but I know that if I don't cooperate it will be the shocks again.

The cold metal is expanding in my limbs, thrusting its sharp edges in my brain.

Slashing the dragon to bits.

"A man wearing a cylindrical coat who is praying with his arms raised. On his side two opposing faces," I say in a very low voice. Whilst what I am seeing is the beast. Asleep with its wings wide open perched on a building reading to take flight.

Dr Fromm brings the first card behind the deck and presents me with another one.

"What do you see?" I want you to leave me alone. You don't understand its power.

This one is a larger black abstract image with some red coloring. "I see a white umbrella in a gray field." I say and nod. I see my hips cracked by the impact with the ground. I see hips with blood stains as if a woman has just birthed a child. That is my mother's blood I can taste metal in my mouth and dragon fire burning in my throat. The dragon is waking and with it the fire that will burn them to ash. I can see their body charred by the fire jet exiting my mouth. First their skin, then their flesh and finally their bones. I have no time for this bullshit. My skin is made impenetrable by steel. My tail swings with destructive force. There is something very intimate I have hooked into. My words are a dragon spears hooked deep inside me. The more I speak the more I feel it tense as if what it is hooked to is resisting the pull upward. The more I want to speak the more it tenses and it hurts. I must take flight.

"Vince. Vince? Are you ok?" Dr. Fromm spears the dragon in midair without camouflaging behind watercolor images. I stare at my wounded hand. When I decide to make eye contact with her I am focusing on her blond hair. I know she wants to invade my mind again.

"Before we finish here can you tell me if you had that dream again? In our last session you talked about saving Caius for murdering his mother. Is there something familiar in this? I want you to know that Dr. Levitt and I believe that Caius is a good man and that you are a good man" I am standing on the balcony in Rome. I am with my mother and I shake my head as she shakes hers.

"You don't agree Vince? is that why you are shaking your head?" I can see her head shake on that balcony. I am shaking with her. I can feel mercury in my arms. My nerves become rods within my flesh. My face flushes when the steel tenses the muscles. My hands cold, liquid and lethal at the touch. Mother's warmth raising the mercuric darkness from my finger, through my arms, inside.

My arteries into my heart. Heat that suffocates my humanity. Only swift action can stop the metallic liquid from taking over my heart. Sudden drop. Push the heat to drop.

My head reaches higher to stop the rising mercury. Dr. Fromm signals Todd to come forward and I am led out of the room. I don't know what I have said but the dragon is now awake and they've must have known. I am being led back into my room. Once inside the door closes gently, with respect. The window is calling, so I get closer to it and look outside. Everything looks the same from here. They sky, the buildings, the cars on the distant highway and that billboard "Family Time Matters." Although they say things change. Not from here they don't. On a table against the wall I see a DVD box set titled Blanc, Bleu and Rouge and a photo of my mother and I with our dog. Ah, when in Rome.

I reach my shoe and find Melissa's list. I must get to Tom Phelps. I place one foot, then the other, on the ground and stand away from the wheelchair. I walk to the loo and detect a small window right above it. I climb on the toilet rim. I unscrew the small square window by sliding my thumb nail in the wedge. I pull my chest to the sill and think of my mother. Probably because of that billboard facing me. 'Family Time Matters.' I push myself out and reach for the drainage pipe. I am unable to hold on as the circumference is too wide for me so I resort to jamming my fingers behind it. As I move down I scrape the back of my palms against the wall. I don't feel pain but when I reach the ground my hands are bleeding. I pull out my sweatshirt and wipe off the blood. I stand still looking out in the garden with only one thought in mind. Get to Tom Phelps.

I make a move. A cold breeze strokes my wounds. At first the cold sensation numbs the burning. But when I put my hands back in my pockets a backdraft effect causes my hands to burn like a motherfucker. My phone vibrates and as I reach for it I brush my hands against the inner linings of my jeans.

"Where are you Vince!?" Dr Levitt asks.

"Can't trust you anymore. You are in this with her." Wind blows echoing in the receiver.

"Vince, listen to me. This is the only place where you can get help. Dr.

Fromm says she has helped people like you before."

"So is that who Dr. Fromm is?" I say. The phone falls from my hand and I freeze.

*Prixus, the Gaul, finishes Vetraites off with a lightning strike. The crowd becomes ecstatic at the sight of the gushing blood. The liquid flows out of the severed neck into the absorbing arena sand. The body and its head are quickly removed. Caius is escorted in again. He takes rapid circular steps to take full advantage of his ankle chains.*

*Micero stands again in the gubernatorial box and calls for the crowd to quiet down.*

*"Fellow Romans, following a great fight I want to call on you to thank the gods for a fruitful outcome. We are all*

*thankful to these great fighters and to the skills they have demonstrated ." The crowd screams the name of Prixus and the whole arena joins in a thundering chorus. Micero sits, and the governor Marcus Augustinus stands and raises his hand.*

*"In front of you is Caius. A roman who lost his way. It is now our turn to grant him death or exile," says the governor.*

*The crowd goes into a hushed frenzy. Consultation erupts in all sections of the circular building. Senators, equites and plebeians.*

*Marcus Augustinus extends his arm again to signal it is time to choose.*

*The gods want their voice to be heard. Cold September drops start falling from the sky. The governor waits patiently for a consensus whilst the plebeians start to scatter. As the rainfall increases, Caius lifts his head toward the sky and smiles.*

When the dream comes to an end I feel empty inside. It's like the after effect of exhaustive crying. No emotions, just a burning sensation in my throat and cold air brushing against the lining of my insides where there is a hole in my chest.

Caius. Who would have known a guy from a fucked up dream would have costed me my sanity. Mors tua vita mea . Your death is my life, as you roman would say. I must find a way to let someone know Caius will be saved. So that this joke I call my life will not be a complete failure. On my terms, though. Melissa will have to pay for what she and her group have done to me and to other people.

I am in my apartment staring outside. Everything looks the same from here. They sky, the buildings, the cars on the distant highway and that billboard "Family Time Matters." Although they say things change. Not from here they don't. I push my face against the cold glass to feel me or the little that is left of me. I grab my phone to check if Byron has read my text. "Yo. I am on my way. Gimme half hour."

He should be here soon. My index has been busy digging into my left thumb's cuticle. Of what is left of it. My brain is telling me that my nail is being slowly pulled off. I look at it but there seems to be nothing wrong with my thumb. I register a force that is lifting my nail up, I register the rawness of the nail bed. I drag myself to the kitchen, pour half a glass of sambuca and mix it with about 40 Xanax drops. I slide my thumb between the index and middle finger to squeeze the force away. Fuck off brain. God it hurts.

I grab my drink and go sit in my revolving lounge chair. I turn on the TV and start channel surfing. I turn it off as everything is so alive, as if I had time. Everything in there wants me to pay attention and stay put. But I can't stay. My die has been cast, motherfuckers. I am of another kind. I am of the 3rd kind. I am between life and nothingness. Finally, now that the screen is off, I see myself. A dark outline inside the box. The buzzer goes off and I look at the outline within the screen. It moves with me.

"Hey man, how you feeling?" Byron asks as he takes his black Goretex Arc'teryx jacket off. I lean back on the chair. Byron comes closer and puts his hand on my shoulder before sitting on Danielle's couch.

"Byron. Thanks for coming."

"Sure man. We going to get through this."

"What makes you think I'll be able to make it?" I smile.

"I spoke to Dr. Levitt. They are looking for you. They are probably on their way here. Why did you run away?"

"Wouldn't you?" I am staring at him as to keep other thoughts away. My nail is throbbing. I surround it with my hand and squeeze hard.

"I don't know. I am sure they will be able to deal with it. You are not really sure it was mind donation, are you?" Byron has spread his arms wide over the couch head rest.

"How do you know about mind-donation?"

"Relax, man. Dr. Levitt told me."

"Is that all he told you?"

"Yes. He told me that you are unwell and that you need treatment. Why aren't you allowing them to help you?"

"Melissa confessed I was part of the mind donor program because they knew I had given up on life."

"What?! Vince are you sure? I mean you are talking about some serious accusation here." Byron brings his hand up to scratch the tip of his nose.

"All I know is that I am going fucking crazy since I met her. She told me I was selected ahead of time. Recruited by my co-worker, Todd."

"Vince. Dr. Levitt, what did he say?" Byron moves away from the head rest and sits at the edge of the sofa.

"He said it could be mind donation."

"So you are not sure?" Byron turns his head left and right to emphasize.

"Byron. For fuck's sake. Both Melissa and Todd have admitted to me that they were using me to regress in time."

"Did they talk of mind donation?"

"No they did not! Fuuuuck!" I grab the glass from the tea table and throw it against the wall. It explodes as if before hitting the wall it self detonated. "You don't believe me, do you? You think I am making this shit up. You think I am hallucinating." I look at the ceiling to find a reason to all of this. I look at the TV screen and at the dark outline. As I see my dark reflection I feel at ease again. I need to be looking both at the screen and at Byron. I need to know I am not fading away.

"Vince of course I believe you. I think you should go to the hospital because you are under a lot of stress. Dr. Levitt told me you should be under medication. Are you taking what he prescribed you?"

"Yes. But I don't think it's working." I laugh as it is easier to let go. Sarcasm is the last defense of the defeated.

"Byron, you are a good man. I thought it since I first met you. What did you think when you met me?" I turn toward the screen and I nod. Never thought I'd be nostalgic of myself.

"Vince, I thought you were and are an interesting person. You have something about you. Something that makes you look out of place. I can't really describe it but when I saw you in that diner you looked like you didn't belong. You were talking to your friend but it felt as though you weren't really there."

"Byron, I have something to leave with you." I get up and walk to the kitchen counter. I grab a pen and write 'Caius is saved in the Coliseum' on a piece of paper. I slip it into an envelope and hand it to him.

"If something happens to me, they will come to you to find out what is written in there . This will also mean that what I told you is true."

Byron takes the envelop and stays seated. Eyes on the blank paper.

"Sure man. I will keep it safe." He grabs his jacket and slides it in the internal pocket.

The pain in my thumb is getting sharper. I frown when a sudden sting punctures the bare raw flesh.

"What's wrong?" Asks Byron.

"Nothing."

"Can I drive you to the hospital?"

"No. First, I need to do one last thing."

# 41

When I get to Tom Phelps' apartment building I am met by a strong paint smell coming from the lobby. I see paint buckets collected in the right corner by the mailboxes. On the opposite side there is a dog leashed to the foot of a lobby couch. It follows me, trying to smell me. When he is close enough the fully extended leash snaps him back to his radius. I start walking up the stairs but part of me warns we will never be able to find him this way. I go back to the intercom, find Tom's name and press the button. The pain underneath my nail is back. The blood pressure constricts and expands nerve endings. "Hello," Tom answers.

"Hey Tom, this is Vince, a friend of Melissa. " I raise my left hand in front of me to cover my dermal exposure.

"Oh, I was not expecting a visit, "says Tom.

"Sorry to drop on you like this. It's about AppYours."
"Ohhh, I see. Come up, come up. 19th floor," says Tom.

Once in the elevator I move into the corner. I hunch my back to fit within the angle where the 2 mirrors meet.

The elevator rises and I feel heavier. It's the inertia of my body that moves whilst standing still. I need to look at the neon light above me to stand erect. The light keeps me reaching for warmth, clarity. "Who is it?" Tom asks dragging the phonetic U from behind the door. "It's Vince."

"Sorry, you catch me in a bad time. Wow they work fast. You are a match from the app? I mean happy for you to come by but as you can see I am not at my best." Tom tries to straighten his shirt by pulling it down over his stomach bulge with his left hand. His right thumb is bandaged. I look at mine, a mirroring mechanism, but the gauze seems to be gone.

Tom holds up a stare as to read what my leanings are. Then slowly rolls his eyes over my body.

"Please come in darling. Don't mind the mess. I have been a bit busy lately," he says. The plump fellow has a hard time opening the door as collected old newspapers lying on the ground get stuck under it. Behind him, piles of newspapers, clothes, boxes, folded bags, and toys. Lots of toys.

"Thanks, Tom. No worries. This is about the app but I am not one of your matches. I am a user who can give you some very important information about it."

"Oh. That's too bad. I am quite excited about this new technology. You know I am as digital as my alarm clock, " says Tom.

"I'll just take 5 minutes of your time." I say.

"Sure. Come in. Here, make yourself comfortable. Can I get you something?" He shows me into the living room and then hobbles his flat butt over to the kitchen. I can fee gaze on me as I make space among the boxes and magazines on the couch. I stand in front of his living room window. I need to focus and stay with my objective. With the reasons I came here for. Yet I feel a pull towards the outside. As if out there my head would get bigger and everything in it would disperse.

"You know, it is very important to look out of the window," says Tom from the kitchen.

"How so?" I see that huge billboard again and read it 'Family Time Matters' to try injecting a memory of my own family.

"Well I do it a lot. I think it is the only time when you can allow thoughts to flow in your head or outside. When you look out there you are making yourself part of the bigger picture. You are not the focus anymore."

I sit and something strikes my attention. A family photo of the size of a poster on the wall in front of me. In the portrait I recognize Tom, at about 20 years of age, a woman who appears to be his mother and a dog. Eerily similar to the one I keep on my bookshelf. As I try to make up a story for the image he comes over with a tray containing a glass of water and some cookies. He sits on the couch and crosses his legs. He then swiftly repositions himself as his legs are too fat to be crossed.

"Ah yes. That's my mommy Danielle, may she rest in peace. She took a leap not long ago," Tom sighs. I find myself trying to formulate my next sentence but I am unable to speak. I feel trapped inside. I can see the window.

The rest of the room has gone dark. I am back in a faraway dream, arguing with Danielle on my balcony.

"Vince. Vince. Hey, are you there? I am sorry. I didn't mean to lay it on you. Have you also lost your mother recently?" Asks Tom when he sees me frozen. He then comes forward and nudges me on the knee.

Like hotwiring a car, Tom's nudge becomes the reality spark that connects with my brain wire. I can feel the electricity ride but there is darkness in my memory. I am trying to remember about my mother and images of Danielle appear. I know she is not her. She is who she is but it doesn't feel right.

"So when did you first get in touch with Melissa?" I ask. I lean forward to reach out for the glass of water and see him stare at my wounded hand.

"Well, she actually got in touch with me at first." His lips are strangely glossy and his nails are longer than you would expect. He continues. "It's a strange story. Actually a weird coincidence, I would say. But if people like us can get together for some fun, why not, right?" He stares at me and rests his hand on my lap. My first instinct is to grab hold of his forearm, twist it around his back and smash his head against the small table in front of us. The center glass would shatter and his throat would slide on the edges of the glass. Thick, rich, pure burgundy blood gushing into a puddle on the dirty carpet.

"Right. Actually, that's not what this is about." Tom was obviously expecting a hook up from Melissa's app. I look at his aorta vein inflating on the side of his neck.

"Oh? Indeed, I did find it strange that you would come directly to my place as I don't remember adding my address to my profile. Then again, I am not very good with technology." He extends his arms over his thighs and leans on them with his elbows, cradling his head. I look past him. My eyes rest on the bookshelf behind where I recognize the Blanc, Bleu and Rouge DVD trilogy.

"Tom. I am here to actually tell you something you might not believe. It may even sound crazy but all I ask you is two minutes of your undivided attention to hear me out."

Tom's expression is blank as he holds his pink Hello Kitty teacup.

"Melissa is using some of the people that join her app to conduct a study."

"I know that." Tom seems relieved. A smile reappears on his face. He takes a sip of his drink. "Listen. It's not about a study or research on people's sexual behaviour through mobile apps as she might have lead you to believe.

The real study begins when you get involved with someone sexually." " Oh, I know that." Tom smiles again and straightens his upper body.

"Please hear me out Tom." I go on telling him about Danielle, the women I met, not remembering about the encounters, discovering about the Mind Donor project without consent and the real goal of the project and its effects on me.

"And now I feel like I am slowly losing my mind. It's like walking into a pond where the water is up to my mouth and I can't breathe. I feel like fading away, like drowning into nonexistence."

Tom has not said a word and has eaten most of the cookies. His voracity is what makes humans so lethal. It appears harmless from here but a bit less so when you look out of the window and millions of Toms are roaming hungry.

"Will you go to the police and tell them what is going on? I have a list with all the people they have targeted." I pull the list out and show it to him." See you and I are both on it. I was hoping you could take it to the police." My hands' trembling has worsened so I lay the list on the table right in front of him.

"Sure, sure. Are you ok? Let me get you some hot chamomile." Tom gets up and disappears into the kitchen. Whilst I look around, my phone rings. It's a message from Melissa asking me to return to the hospital. As I turn back towards the kitchen, I hear the bathroom door close. I wait for Tom to come out and discuss with me how he will reach out to the police. I am about to stand up to check on him when the building alarm goes off. The couch, the deafening alarm sound, me trying to persuade Tom, strike as more than a mere feeling of Deja-vu. I jump up and sprint to the bathroom to check on Danielle. I mean on Tom. I knock on the door. No reply. I rush back into the living room and head for the balcony. A flame of anxiety ignites inside me as I approach the sliding door. I walk out and instinctively look down but no one is there . I mean, there are some people but no one lying on the ground with an exploded skull and chest. I must leave. I retreat inside and as I come close to the entrance door the alarm goes off.

# 42

When I place my hand on the doorknob I hear voices approach. Someone is outside the door. I lean closer and I recognize Todd's, Dr. Levitt's and Melissa's voices. I surprise myself as I feel a smile come over my face. I stand still. The round doorknob slowly turns. My thoracic diaphragm expands as if going deep into my core to pull out a truth that's been there all along, compressed down in my gut by a pounding sense of inadequacy. Like a prisoner born away from any human contact. Able to connect only through the most basic emotions of anger and lust.

*"Vince I have let you do your own thing and look where it has gotten you. Can't you tell that you are disappearing? This is why I am here now. To take care of baby boy" "You are just a thought. Mommy is dead!"*

*"I am not a thought! I am Danielle! Did you think I would just disappear ? Do you want the panic, the fear to continue? You know where this is leading to. A psychiatric ward for the rest of your life, if you are lucky."*

*"Mother?! I, I, I am not yours anymore! It's my life and you will not take over again."*

*"I am sorry. Now it's time for my Vince. The one I molded. The one that stands up for what I believe in. No matter the consequences."*

With simple and methodical movements I slide the balcony door open again. I lean with my back against the railing so I can watch them approach.

I turn around, push up on my toes and as I tilt my head backward I see them rush toward me. Everything looks the same from here. They sky, the buildings, the cars on the distant highway and that billboard "Family Time Matters." Although they say things change. Not from here they don't.

Tom needs to catch his breath after walking down 19 floors. When he exits the building, he flows into something that seems to be causing quite a commotion. A crying woman comes away from the crowd, holding her hands over her face. Using his chubby hands, Tom pushes right through the crowd to discover the man from his apartment shattered on the ground.

# 43

I hear a loud thump, as if something has just hit my window. I get off the bed. My brain is turning on itself. I feel tumbling forward as though the ground were tilting. I sit down again.

Where am I? I was just falling off a building.

I rub my hands over my face and press against the pressure pushing from inside. I'm startled by a loud noise I can't place. It seems to be an alarm.

I head toward the window. Out on the balcony a bird is laying on the ground. I try to make sense of what I am seeing. I stare at the bird. I wonder what I should do. I want to open the window. I reach out for the handle but it is locked. I try to force it.

The bird regains consciousness. I watch it get back up, stumble and fly away.

I turn around when I hear a knock. Dr. Fromm comes in with a small cup in her hand. The other hand is in her pocket, which makes me suspicious. I focus on the pocket. Then, she pulls out a mobile phone. It doesn't reassure me.

She asks me to drink from the cup. I do as I'm told. I know Todd is outside the door. And Todd equals electrocution.

I drink and my mind turns into a sail filled by energy and desire. Desire to reach humanity.

"Vince you want to tell me how you feel?"

"I am alive. Caius is alive."

**~THE END~**

CPSIA information can be obtained
at www.ICGtesting.com
Printed in the USA
BVHW090046130822
644458BV00013B/1131